The
TREASURE
UNDER THE jam
Factory

CHRISSIE
SAINS

ILLUSTRATED BY
JENNY
TAYLOR

Welcome to WILLOWDEN GREEN

M'LAYS JAM!

M'LAYS JAM

CHAPTER ONE

The village of Willowden Green buzzed with rumours about McLay's jam factory.

Something funny was going on up there.

Something strange.

Well, something stranger than usual, anyway. McLay's jam factory had always been a *bit* strange.

For a start, the factory was kept in *absolute secrecy*.

Bullet-proof glass.

Alarms on every door.

And a massive sign that said:

THIS IS A STRICTLY NO STROBBERY ZONE.

Nonetheless, rumours had dribbled out like drips of jam on the edge of the jar.

The villagers had heard about the rollercoaster that ran all the way around the factory, the fountain that trickled three flavours of jam, and the giant robotic hands and tools that made it all.

The factory produced flavours like Electrifying Elderberry, where just one mouthful would make your hair stand on end for the rest of the day.

Or Sherbet Lemon Fizz, a flavour so tinglingly tickly that one nibble would cause a giggling fit that lasted an hour.

Not to mention Racing Runner Bean. A jam that had actually been banned at school sports day after Usain Whizz told everyone that it was the secret formula behind his annual win at the egg-and-spoon race.

How did that astonishing factory keep producing such magnificent jam inventions? And, more importantly, *who* came up with all of the incredible ideas?

Hushed whispers raced around the playground of Willowden Green School with various theories.

"It's got to be a wizard," whispered little George Baker. "They're using magic."

"No way!" snapped Lucy Dunning. "It's Santa's elves! They don't have anything to do in the summer, so they go to work in McLay's Jam!"

"You're both wrong," piped up Oti Messoud. "I know *exactly* who it is!"

The children all leaned in to listen as
Oti cupped her hand over her mouth and
whispered dramatically, "They're *aliens*. They
make the jam using special alien powers."

"Why don't you just ask Scooter?" asked a
rather clever young boy called Joshua Small.
"He must know! He lives there after all."

The children all turned to look at Scooter
McLay as he walked across the playground.
His bog brush orange hair sticking up from his
head. His shoulder covered in jam tart crumbs.
His left shoe a little larger to
allow for his leg splint.

"Nah." Lucy shook
her head decisively.
"He'd *never* tell."

Then, three months ago, McLay's Jam had mysteriously closed. The non-stop whirring and whizzing and whooshing of the factory chimneys had fallen silent and still.

Shortly afterwards, there'd been an announcement in the paper:

It was all very odd. Daffy herself seemed to have mysteriously left town. No one had seen sight nor sound of her, nor her guinea pig with his white coat and bad attitude. Not that anyone really minded. Her doughnuts tasted like cardboard and she wasn't very nice, unlike the McLays, who might be a bit secretive but were friendly about it at least.

The villagers watched as one delivery truck after another arrived at the village, turning merrily up the little dirt track towards the old doughnut factory carrying all sorts of strange things.

Seven truckloads of compost.

Huge glass panels.

Even a truck full of banana trees!

And *that* was when the most exciting thing in the entire history of Willowden Green happened.

A poster went up outside the village hall.

A poster inviting the entire village to a **GRAND REOPENING** party at the new premises of the factory!

Squeals of excitement spread through the village like wildfire.

They were finally allowed in! What tantalizing treats would be in store for them? What delectable delights?

And it was *tonight*?

Within seconds the entire village had scattered like a herd of goats. They bolted back home to dust off their tuxedos and ball gowns in preparation for the wondrous night ahead.

All except for one villager, that is.

Perry Pincher stared at the poster, his eyes twinkling with malice as he twizzled his pencil-thin moustache villainously.

This was *just* the opportunity he'd been waiting for.

He tore the poster from the noticeboard, turned on his heel and began tap-dancing his way home with a wide smile, his gold tooth glinting in the sunlight. He stopped outside the door of a small antiques shop, smoothed down his velvet jacket and sashayed inside, wiggling his hips to the jingle of the bell.

"Colonel Pom Pom!" he called. "I've finally found us a way into that factory! There'll be no more petty thieving for us! We're going to be millionaires!"

"**Meep?**" A small grey ferret poked his head out from a jewellery box, his arms covered in gold rings. He stuffed them into a small bum bag he was wearing, licked his paws and smoothed his whiskers, then fox-trotted, (or rather ferret-trotted) delightedly towards Perry.

"Those daft McLays have invited the whole village to see inside. Don't I always say, all good things come to those who wait?"

"**Meep!**" Colonel Pom Pom held up a ring with a furry grin.

"Ha! Of course, of course, all *gold* things come to those who wait! Good one, Colonel Pom Pom." They sniggered together like two cheeky schoolboys.

"Shall we?" Perry and Colonel Pom Pom shimmied their way towards a short stone staircase at the back of the shop, which led down to a large, padlocked door. Perry pulled a brass key out of his pocket, unlocked the door and opened it with a flourish. "Ta-da!" He clicked his heels and stepped inside.

The room was filled with boxes of plunder that Perry had pilfered. Pocket

watches, gold rings, books, photos, teddy bears, even an old television that Perry had found in a skip filled with Daffy Dodgy's old stuff.

Perry ignored it all and marched straight towards the back of the room to his most valuable find of all … half a faded, yellowing map pinned to the wall.

"The entrance is *somewhere* inside that old doughnut factory." He stuck the Grand Reopening poster to the wall next to it, before turning back to the map and rubbing his long finger thoughtfully along the torn edge of the page. "It would be so much easier if we had the whole thing." He sighed.

"**Meep!**" Colonel Pom Pom wiggled his nose significantly.

"That's true." Perry gave Colonel Pom Pom's nose a fond tap. "With your nose for treasure, we don't need it." He turned back towards the poster with renewed gusto. "Tonight, we'll find that treasure and we'll nab it!"

"**Meep!**" Colonel Pom Pom twirled delightedly on the spot as Perry step-ball-changed beside him.

"First Captain DodgyBeard's treasure, then on to the best treasure of all, the *One Owner and Their Pet Dance Championship* crown! This is our year!" His smile dropped. "It does mean we'll have to go inside that rotten jam factory though. We've had three blissful months without the stench seeping out. If only it could stay closed for ever." His moustache twitched. "Wait a second! Colonel Pom Pom, I've just had an idea." Perry rubbed his hands together gleefully. "Maybe we should sabotage the factory while we're at it! A few bricks in the machinery ought to..."

"Sabotage *what* factory, Uncle Perry?"

"Gah!" Perry jumped.

A young girl stood with her hands on her hips in the cellar doorway behind him. She wore dungarees that were a little on the big side, plimsolls and mismatched socks: one red and one green.

"Oh, it's *you*." He rolled his eyes. "Still here then?"

"Well, I do live here, Uncle Perry." Cat Pincher pulled a jam sandwich out of her dungaree front pocket and took a large bite.

"Urgh! Get it away! Get it away!" Perry flapped his arms towards her. "It *smells*!" He pulled a clothes peg from his pocket and shoved it

on the end of his schnozzle as he shuffled
her back up the stairs to the shop and
locked the cellar door behind them.
"It's stinky and slimy and sticky
and yucky!" He glared at Cat.

"Have you even tried it?" Cat
spoke with her mouth full.

"Of course not! Why would I *try* it? It's
got *fruit* in it! You're a child, aren't you? I
thought you'd understand *that* at least!"

"Dad says I should always try things before
I make my mind up about whether or not I like
them." Cat took another bite.

"Yes, that sounds exactly like the sort of
thing my goody-goody-for-nothing brother
would say," Perry muttered.

"Hey, what's Mum's jewellery box doing in
here?" Cat pointed to the counter where the
jewellery box that Colonel Pom Pom had been
inside just moments ago was sitting.

"What?" Perry grabbed it and shoved it behind his back. "I don't know what you're talking about." He flashed Cat his most oily smile.

"And where's Mr Jammy, my favourite teddy?" Cat continued suspiciously. "He wasn't in my bed this morning."

Perry's eyes darted towards the cellar door, then over to Colonel Pom Pom.

"How should we know?" They both shrugged not-so-innocently.

"Mum and Dad should never have asked you to take care of the shop." Cat's eyes narrowed. "By the time they get back there won't be anything left to sell."

"Oh, don't worry little Kitty Cat, there'll be plenty of this old toot left for them." Perry curled his lip as he peered around the shop. "Millionaires like Colonel Pom Pom and I don't need to bother with this sort of junk."

Colonel Pom Pom pulled a small silver thimble from his bum bag, poked his tongue out at Cat and flung it dismissively over his shoulder.

"Except…" Cat crossed her arms. "Well, you're *not* a millionaire." She raised her eyebrows. "Are you?"

"Not yet." Perry gave his moustache an especially villainous twizzle as he glanced sideways at the cellar door, then turned back to Cat with a confident sneer.

"But I soon will be."

Scooter McLay stood in the centre of the new jam factory and beamed at the sight that surrounded him. Everything was ready for the Grand Reopening tonight and it was going to be *amazing*.

For years, Scooter had kept his identity as the Chief Inventor at McLay's Jam top secret.

It hadn't exactly been easy. Especially when he'd overheard the hushed whispers and wild theories in the school playground.

But he'd never heard anyone guess at the truth. They'd suggested magic, elves, even *aliens*! And although Scooter couldn't hide a secret smile at that particular idea (after all, he'd tried using alien technology not so long ago and it had turned out to be one whole heap of trouble) it still stung, just a little, that they hadn't wondered if it might actually be him.

Scooter knew why.

The kids at school could see the crumbs on his shoulder, the splint on his left leg and his halo of bright ginger hair. But they couldn't see what was inside: the buzz, the whizz and the fizz of all the ideas and calculations that shot around inside his head, like a swarm of bees that had eaten thirty-seven-and-a-half packets of popping candy.

You had to be a very special someone to be able to see *that*.

You see, when Scooter McLay was first born, it had taken eight whole minutes before he took his first breath.

In those eight long minutes, as he hung between life and death, his brain had somehow developed hyper-creativity.

It had led to another condition too, called cerebral palsy.

Cerebral palsy was different for everyone but for Scooter it meant that the muscles on his left side were a little stiff and he wore an uncomfortable splint on his left leg to stop his foot from dragging. Scooter was OK with that; it was part of him. And anyway, he had other things to think about, like his latest idea, or lately, tonight's Grand Reopening.

After tonight, it wouldn't matter what you could see, everyone would *know* what he could do.

Because Scooter was going to show them *everything*!

And he could not wait.

When they had first taken over the old doughnut factory, it had been an uninspiring, unloved and unhygienic building. But Scooter had found an old wishing well with a small wild strawberry plant growing inside, and that was when he had his most amazing idea *ever*.

Why not grow the fruit they needed for their jam *inside* the factory? After all, the very best jam came from the freshest fruit. If they could take off the old roof and replace it with a glass dome, they could turn it into their very own tropical greenhouse, increasing jam flavour by 63.4%!

His parents had taken a little convincing. How would Scooter grow plants in amongst the machinery? And how could he keep things clean? But Scooter was as determined as he was creative, and after three months of planning, preparing and problem solving, he'd turned the factory into a tropical jam-making *paradise*.

Banana trees lined the walkways. Luscious green strawberry plants covered the walls. Huge hedgerows of blueberry bushes, raspberry canes and trunks of

Brussels sprouts mingled amongst pipes, pistons, pulleys and pumps. And all the while giant robotic hands and tools beavered away, spraying, picking, supervising and sorting to the musical sound of jam jars tinkling along on conveyor belts.

There was just one part of the factory that remained the same: the huge tower that loomed darkly over the building like a great shadow, topped with the words *Dodgy Doughnuts*.

The Dodgy Tower was the only part of the factory that Daffy hadn't handed over to the McLays. Scooter was itching to take down that rubbish neon sign and replace it with a bright flag that said *McLay's Jam*. But he didn't dwell on it. He'd been far too busy filling the new factory with his most exciting jam flavours and inventions *ever*.

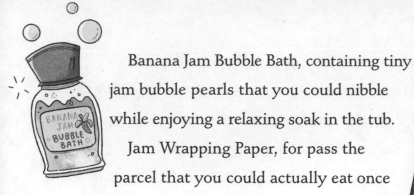

Banana Jam Bubble Bath, containing tiny jam bubble pearls that you could nibble while enjoying a relaxing soak in the tub.

Jam Wrapping Paper, for pass the parcel that you could actually eat once you'd unwrapped a layer.

Even Hiccup-free Huckleberry Jam to cure hiccups.

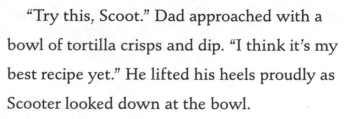

And there were so many more!

Tonight had to be *perfect*.

"Try this, Scoot." Dad approached with a bowl of tortilla crisps and dip. "I think it's my best recipe yet." He lifted his heels proudly as Scooter looked down at the bowl.

Scooter didn't like to say anything. After all, Dad had spent weeks in the kitchen testing out new recipes ready for the party. But crisps and dip seemed a bit … well, a bit ordinary really. He picked one up, dipped it into the oozy salsa and popped it in his mouth, with a satisfying crunch.

His eyes opened wide as he realized that the crisp was made of hard toffee. And the dip was toffee-apple jam! It was delicious. He dunked another. "Wow, Dad, these are incredible!"

"All the food at the Grand Reopening will be jam-themed." Dad's cheeks glowed proudly as he pulled a menu out of his apron pocket. "We've got Lemon Jam Fizz to drink, glow-in-the-dark jam sandwiches, Bubble Gum Jam Sausages and Smoking Strawberry Jam Ice Cream. Not to mention my light-as-air floating jam tarts!" He brushed down his apron with a satisfied smile. "Turns out I can be pretty inventive myself in the kitchen."

"Well, we've been learning from the best." Mum nudged Scooter fondly as she pocketed

31

her spanner and nabbed a crisp.

"Right then, that's the tools all programmed to start serving food at precisely 6 p.m." She pulled on a rope to lift a net full of jam balloons up to the ceiling. "And talking of floating jam tarts, Scoot – where's Fizzbee?"

"She's been working on the new treetop canopy bridge." Scooter looked at the ropes and wooden planks, nestled among the banana trees overhead. "It's increased the rollercoaster thrill factor by 72.9%!"

Right on cue, a jam tart whooshed high above their heads, a tiny orange hand waving from over the pastry rim as it darted towards them.

Scooter waved back eagerly.

Fizzbee was his best friend in all

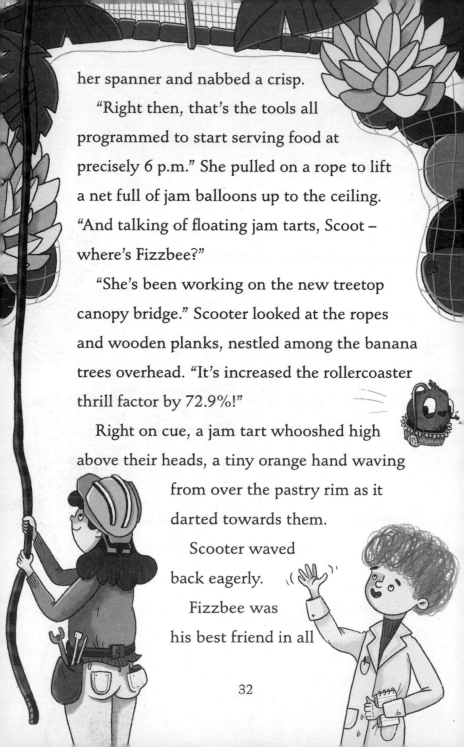

the world … maybe even the universe, too, seeing as she was actually an alien. But as the little jam tart drew closer, Scooter could see her tiny orange brow wrinkled with concern as she pointed urgently towards the Dodgy Tower. "Scooter!" she called. "There is something that Fizzbee must—"

A light above made them all look up together.

The Dodgy Doughnuts sign blinked once, then twice, then…

Click.

Whirrrrrr.

Switched *on*.

"Scooter, the door!" Fizzbee pointed from her jam tart towards the Dodgy Tower.

Scooter craned his neck to see the door of the Dodgy Tower. Normally it was covered with chains and padlocks, but these were nowhere to be seen and the door was very slightly ajar. One lone guinea pig dropping lay on the floor.

"You don't think?" Mum froze, another crisp halfway towards her mouth.

"It can't be!" Dad shuddered.

Creeeeeeaaaaaaaaaaaak.

The door slowly began to open and a long, dark shadow filled the doorway.

CHAPTER THREE

"Cooooo-eeeeeeee!"

"Squee–eeeeeeeak!"

It was a voice and a squeak that made
Scooter's blood run cold.

"We're baaaack!"

"It can't be!" Mum recoiled.

"No! Please, not them!" Dad dropped the
bowl of crisps on the floor, as in strolled

Daffy Dodgy, her brown velour tracksuit shimmering in the neon light of the *Dodgy Doughnuts* sign and her fat white guinea pig, Boris, snuggled smugly in a baby carrier on her front.

"Thanks for doing up *my* factory." She raised her eyebrows as she lifted a large remote control, a slow smile creeping onto her face.

"What do you mean *your* factory?" Scooter stepped forwards as Daffy pressed a button on the remote control.

CLICK. CLICK. CLICK. Whirrrrr.

For a moment the *Dodgy Doughnuts* sign stuttered and stammered, shunted and shook until finally it *changed* before their very eyes.

Scooter blinked.

"I was never seriously going to give it
to you." Daffy's smile turned to a giggle as
she pointed her thin finger towards them.
"I can't believe you losers actually fell for it!"
She began hopping from one foot to the other
in delight at her cunning.

"*What?*" Scooter's mum stepped forwards.
"You have to be joking!"

"Too right!" Scooter's dad pulled his wallet
out of his trouser pocket, opened it and took
out a folded postcard. "You signed the factory
over to us! You wrote it in black and white on
this!" He unfolded the postcard, and held it up
triumphantly. "You see! It says it right—" He
stopped talking as he looked at the postcard,
his face slowly draining of colour.

"I knew you'd say that." Daffy snatched the postcard out of his hand. "That's why I used disappearing ink when I wrote it." She let out a delighted squeal as she began ripping it up before their eyes, dropping it to the floor like confetti. "The fact is, I still own the factory."

She pulled out an old yellowing scroll from beside Boris in the carrier, brushed off a guinea pig poo pellet and opened it up for them to see. "It's all right here on the deeds. *I* own the factory and *nobody* else. See for yourself." She rolled it back up and handed it over to Scooter's mum as Dad scrabbled on the floor to pick up the pieces of postcard.

"What do you mean?" Scooter stared hard at Daffy, a large lump in his throat. "Was it a trick? You just pretended to give us the factory so I'd put all of my inventions in it … so you could steal them? And call it *Dodgy Jam*?"

"Well… I…" Daffy looked uncomfortable

for a moment. Her mouth opened as if she was about to say something, then clamped shut again. She looked up at the *Dodgy Jam* sign, before finally meeting Scooter's burning gaze with a shrug. "It's not stealing if it was mine the whole time, is it?"

"**Squeak**." Boris raised his eyebrows with a haughty nod.

"Anyway, it's not my fault." Her face hardened. "You shouldn't have been so gullible."

"**Squeak**." Boris nodded again as Daffy surveyed the factory with a satisfied smile.

"Looks like everything's ready for my Grand Reopening tomorrow night. And now you'd better shove off back to your factory." She pointed towards the old building next door, the words *McLay's Jam* hanging lopsidedly over the door. "Because everything here –" she grinned as she spread her arms wide around her – "is *mine*."

McLay's Jam (the first) was only a short
walk from the premises of the newly named
Dodgy Jam, but it felt like a long one. Normally
Scooter would take the rollercoaster to get
between the factories. After all, he and his
parents still lived in the flat above the original
factory. And he still did his best thinking
in the old Jam Inventions Lab, where he'd
come up with some of his best jam flavours
and ideas.

It was for this reason that he headed
straight there.

Because if there was ever a time that he
needed to do his best thinking, it was right
now.

His mind raced with ideas as he stepped
through the steel security door into the lab,
Fizzbee hovering loyally by his shoulder.
His parents followed behind.

"We've got to do something." Scooter stood in front of his workbench, his hands on his hips as Fizzbee landed on the table and Mum and Dad sat down quietly on the stools. "She can't just come in here and call *our* factory Dodgy Jam and say it's still hers!"

Dad emptied the tiny pieces of postcard onto the workbench, his head shaking in disbelief as he tried to jigsaw them back together. "We've been doing it up for *months*!" Mum stared glassy-eyed at the scroll in her hands. "And we can't let her host our Grand Reopening. She didn't make anything in that factory! It's just..." Scooter stopped.

Why weren't Mum and Dad agreeing with him?

"*… the worst name for a jam factory ever!*" Fizzbee slammed her fist down.

"Yeah!" Scooter smiled at Fizzbee gratefully. He could always rely on her to agree with him, even though that wasn't *quite* what he had been going to say.

Mum and Dad shared a sad look, before Mum finally met his eyes.

"I'm sorry, Scoot." She looked at the tiny pieces of postcard on the workbench. "But we don't have anything to say that the factory actually belongs to us. Daffy tricked us. We've done it all up for nothing."

"It could be worse." Dad gave Scooter a well-meaning smile. "At least we've still got the flat, plus *this* factory."

Scooter sighed.

It was true.

The original factory was smaller and a bit less up-to-date. It might not have his coolest inventions in it, but it *did* have his first rollercoaster ... and it still had the fountain that trickled three flavours of jam. It even had giant robotic tools and the wasp-testing tunnel.

But it didn't have the huge glass dome.

Or the banana trees.

Or the treetop canopy.

And it was far too small to host a Grand Reopening.

Scooter really had been especially looking forward to that.

Plus, it didn't have all of the new jam flavours and inventions that he and Fizzbee had developed *together*. Scooter watched as Fizzbee tried to help Dad put the postcard back together. Fizzbee had turned out to be a great jam inventor. She—

Wait a second!

A small idea bee buzzed inside Scooter's brain.

When Fizzbee had first arrived, she'd brought with her a whole suitcase of alien inventions that could do almost *anything*.

His eyes darted towards it now, wedged on the top shelf above them, with a sign propped in front of it in Mum's handwriting.

He glanced at Fizzbee. Her head was raised, a wide grin on her face. She seemed to know *exactly* what he was thinking. She stood on the desk taut with anticipation, her small body beginning to glow, like a tiny excitable bomb that might explode at any second.

Scooter held up his hand with a small nod. If they were going to persuade Mum and Dad to let them use anything from Fizzbee's suitcase of inventions, then they would need to approach the subject carefully. After all, it wasn't so long ago that Fizzbee's suitcase had led to less than amazing results involving a giant guinea pig, a teeny tiny Scooter and a lot of damage to the factory.

"I've got an idea," Scooter began. "And hear me out before you make your mind up. What about—"

"*We must use Fizzbee's suitcase of inventions!*" Fizzbee exploded with a high-pitched squeal.

"What?" Dad's head jerked up in surprise.

"There might be something in there that could help!" Scooter added hastily. "Like a potion to change Daffy's mind, or maybe there's a way to send her and Boris somewhere else. Then at least we could still have the Grand Reopening and it would give us some time to figure out a plan!" He turned to Fizzbee, ignoring the stony expression on his parents' faces. "Do you have anything like that in your suitcase, Fizzbee? Or, you know, something else that might be useful?"

Fizzbee thought for a moment, but before she had a chance to say anything, Mum stood up and put her hand on Scooter's shoulder.

46

"You know how we feel about that suitcase, Scoot." She gave a sad but firm shake of her head.

Scooter slumped down onto his workbench stool and rested his head wearily on the backrest as Mum unrolled the scroll that Daffy had given to her. She laid it on the workbench, pinning it down at each corner with a jam jar. It was old and yellowing and torn on one side. There was even some kind of faded drawing beneath the words of the deeds. There was no doubt about it. The factory belonged to Daffy.

"These old deeds seem watertight." Mum pulled her phone out of her pocket and took a photo. "But your dad and I will see a lawyer. I won't take the deeds, they look like they might fall apart any second, but I'll show them this photo. Perhaps there's a way to take back your inventions at least." Mum looked out of the window towards the tower looming above them, the words *Dodgy Jam* flashing brightly above it. "I don't think we'll ever get the factory back. If only we could just buy it from Daffy before she has a chance to open it."

"Well, let's do that!" Scooter jumped up, his heart soaring for a moment.

"Oh Scoot, I'm sorry." Mum's face fell. "We don't have the money. Not unless you find a nice big stack of buried treasure." She smiled sadly. "But we both know that's never going to happen."

CHAPTER FOUR

Little did Scooter know that treasure was far closer than he could possibly have imagined. In fact, if he could only have seen inside the cellar of the Pinchers' antiques store at that exact moment, then he would have found the answer to all of his problems.

But it was Cat Pincher who was currently standing outside the locked cellar door. She wiggled a small hair clip in the padlock until she heard a satisfying click. She put the clip back in her hair, quietly pulled open the door and tiptoed inside.

You see, Cat was as resourceful as Scooter was determined. With the help of her trusty *How to Be a Spy* pocketbook, Cat had trained herself on how to pick a lock, how to pick a pocket and how to pick out Uncle Perry's lies.

Cat was absolutely certain that Uncle Perry and Colonel Pom Pom had nabbed her teddy bear, Mr Jammy.

Ever since they'd moved in to help mind the shop while her parents were away on an archaeological dig, she'd watched as they swiped the family valuables from her home. For a while, Cat had let their pilfering ways slide. After all, her parents would be back any day. They'd soon put a stop to Uncle Perry's thieving.

But stealing Mr Jammy, her oldest teddy, from her *actual* bed?

Well, that was taking things too far.

She'd had Mr Jammy since the day she was born. He might be a bit old and yeah, maybe Cat didn't play with him much any more, but he was important. And Cat wasn't going to let Uncle Perry take him.

As her eyes adjusted to the dim light of the cellar, she searched for the red and green of Mr Jammy's socks, which matched her own. It wasn't long before she struck lucky. She marched over to a box full of teddy bears, one tiny red socked leg poking out. She reached inside, pulled a small brown bear from the box and hugged him tight.

Her gaze fell on half an old map pinned to the wall.

Ye Wishing

Here lies ye olde treasure of Captain DodgyBeard

Now, Cat wasn't just resourceful, she was smart, too. As she saw the map, she couldn't help remembering Uncle Perry's talk of becoming a millionaire.

So, his plan was to find some old treasure?

Her eyes flicked towards the Grand Reopening poster pinned to the wall next to the map and she quickly put two and two together. It was the perfect way for Uncle Perry to get inside! And hadn't he said something about a sabotage?

"Well, I can't let him get away with that," she muttered as she unpinned the map from the wall and shoved it down her red sock. She turned on her heel and marched out of the door. She had to warn the McLays – and fast.

Meanwhile, back at the jam inventions lab, Scooter waved his parents goodbye. He waited until they were out of sight, then turned back to Fizzbee, his mouth set in a grim line of determination.

"We're not going to let Daffy take our factory." He glanced up to where the suitcase of alien inventions sat between two jars of jam, each marked with a warning sign.

"Are you thinking what I'm thinking?" His eyes met with Fizzbee's as he nodded his head towards the shelf.

Fizzbee paused for a moment. She glanced up to the shelf, then back to Scooter.

"Is Scooter thinking that we give Daffy a Shrinking Strawberry Jam sandwich and shrink Daffy to size of a pea, then *squish her like a bug*?" Fizzbee stamped her foot hard as she spoke.

"Err." Scooter stepped back. "Not exactly."

"Ah." Fizzbee nodded sagely. "Is Scooter thinking that we should eat growing jam and become like giants, so that we can sit on Daffy and *squish her like a bug*?" This time she body-slammed her bottom down like a tiny ping-pong-sized wrestler.

"Nooooooo." Scooter couldn't help giggling. "I'm not really thinking about bug squishing."

"Tssk." Fizzbee shrugged. "Then Scooter is thinking that we should use Fizzbee's case to make a *new* invention to stop Daffy."

"Now you've got it!" Scooter smiled. "So, what have you got up there?"

Fizzbee hovered up towards the suitcase, heaved it onto her jam tart and drifted unsteadily back down to Scooter's workbench. She lifted open the lid to reveal jars and test tubes of brightly coloured liquids and potions. Fizzbee rummaged around inside before pulling out a small shaker filled with a silvery, sugar-like powder.

"Wow, what does that one do?" Scooter asked.

"Anti-gravity powder. To make you fly! We give this to Daffy and she floats up to space." Fizzbee pointed up to the sky. "Space is very nice. Daffy would like it there."

Her face lit up. "Poof. Problem solved!"

"Err. Well, actually, humans can't breathe in space." Scooter cleared his throat with a small awkward cough. "So maybe we should keep looking? What about something to help change her mind? Do you have anything like that?"

Fizzbee rummaged around in her suitcase again. This time she pulled out a shaker of what looked just like hundreds and thousands sprinkles. As Scooter peered at them, he felt warm and fuzzy and...

"This is verrry powerful." Fizzbee pulled it back a little warily. "This is Friendship Sprinkles."

"Friendship Sprinkles?" Scooter stared at the little jar in Fizzbee's hand. "What do you mean?"

"These sprinkles make friendships much stronger," Fizzbee explained. "If Daffy eats Friendship Sprinkles, she would want to make

Scooter her *best* friend! She would do anything you asked."

"Wow, really?" Scooter thought about it. Just a shake of those sprinkles and he could get the factory back! All of their problems would be over. "So, if Daffy had some of this, she'd sign the factory back to us, just because I asked her to?"

"Maybe." Fizzbee thought about it. "Except, it only works if she already likes you a *little bit*." Fizzbee indicated with her forefinger and thumb.

"Oh." Scooter scratched his head.

"Well, I don't think she likes me *at all*. I mean, she can't, can she? Not after the trick she's played on us!" He pointed back at the suitcase. "Maybe we should try something else. What about that thing Mum said? You know, that we could buy the factory back from Daffy? Do you have anything that can get us enough money? Like…" He scratched his head. "I dunno, maybe a potion that can find gold or a money tree seed or something like that?"

"Hmmm." Fizzbee turned back to the suitcase and rooted around inside, muttering.

No.

No.

No.

She looked up and shook her head. "Fizzbee does not have a potion that can find gold."

"Hold on!" Scooter cried. "Did you say *Reappearing Potion*?"

"Yes." Fizzbee pulled out a vial of black liquid while Scooter pointed excitedly at the torn pieces of postcard Dad had left on his workbench.

"Maybe we could use that on the postcard!" He beamed. "Do you think it would put the pieces back together, too?"

"Fizzbee is not sure." Fizzbee shook her head doubtfully as she took a small pipette from the Reappearing Potion and held it over the pieces of postcard on top of the old scroll. "But Fizzbee is thinking this is our only plan at the moment." She dripped a tiny drop onto the postcard.

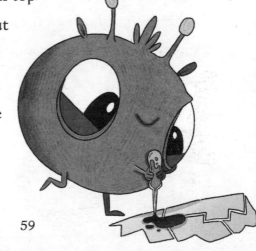

For a moment, the black liquid pooled on the pieces of postcard. Then, it slowly slid off and began soaking into the old scroll below it.

"Hold on, what's happening?" Scooter watched in amazement as small black lines began to dash and dart and, finally, *draw* across the old scroll. He swept the postcard pieces to one side to look closer. Where there had been a faded picture under the words of the contract, somehow the Reappearing Potion seemed to be making the lines darker. In fact, the wording of the deeds was slowly being scrubbed out and replaced with twirly old lettering and pictures.

There was a compass on the right-hand corner of the page.

To the left, a skull and crossbones.

Scooter's mouth fell open as the black lines continued to scrawl across the page, revealing half the plans of a building. From the torn edge of the page, there was half a circle labelled *Olde Well* and a large cross in one room, with an arrow pointing towards it.

"I think this might be a map!" Scooter's eyes opened wide as Fizzbee came to hover beside him. "A really old map." He peered down at the skull and crossbones. "You don't think it could be a *treasure map*, do you?"

"Oh brilliant, you found the other half!" To Scooter's absolute amazement, a girl swung down from a pipe in the ceiling. She put her hands on the inventions table, somersaulted backwards and landed on her scruffy plimsolls in front of them. "I was just coming to talk to you about that."

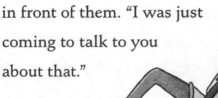

Scooter stared at the girl in front of him.

"Errrrr. What? How?" He scratched his head.

"Don't you make *one* move!" Fizzbee zipped between them, her eyes narrowed as she brandished a blueberry between her thumb and forefinger. "Or we squish you ..." She squeezed the blueberry between her two tiny fingers.

Pfffffff.

A small puff of air escaped from the blueberry.

"... like a BUG!"

Fizzbee squished the blueberry harder.

Pffffffffff.

The intruder raised one eyebrow.

Fizzbee put the blueberry on her jam tart and lifted her little foot.

"LIKE A BUG!" She stamped down hard.

The blueberry popped out from under her foot, whizzed towards the girl and bounced off her forehead with all the mighty force of a ... well, of a slightly wrinkled and altogether completely harmless blueberry.

BOP.

"Argh! I've been blueberried!" the girl cried as she began writhing around on the floor,

63

pretending to wrestle with the blueberry. The corner of Fizzbee's mouth twitched a little and Scooter couldn't help giggling. Whoever this girl was, she was quite funny. But that didn't explain what she was doing here. Or how she'd got in. And it definitely didn't explain how she knew about the map.

The girl stood up, popped the blueberry in her mouth with a friendly wink and held out her hand.

"I'm Cat." She smiled.

Scooter looked down at her hand. He had to admit, for someone who'd just broken in, she didn't seem like a *typical* burglar.

"I'm Scooter." He took her hand and shook it, careful to avoid being *too* friendly. He didn't entirely trust her just yet. Fizzbee, on the other hand, seemed to have decided that she liked the girl. She flew her jam tart just an arm's length from Cat's face, held her gaze for a moment, then chuckled with delight before landing on top of her head.

"And that's Fizzbee." Scooter cleared his throat. "She's not exactly from around here."

"*Alien?*" Cat whispered. Scooter nodded in reply. "Thought so." She gave Fizzbee a friendly little pat.

"So, what are you doing here?" Scooter looked up to the pipes above. "And ... how did you get in?"

"Well, believe me, it wasn't easy. I had to squeeze myself through some tight spots." Cat held a book up for them to see. "Luckily I had this to help me! And as for why I'm here, well, I came to warn

65

you about my Uncle Perry. And also, to show you this map!" She bent down and pulled the yellowing scroll from her red sock. "I didn't realize you already had the other half!"

She unrolled the scroll and laid it carefully on the workbench, matching the ripped edges. Almost as soon as the two halves met, the Reappearing Potion darted towards the centre. The black liquid began to stitch the edges together like the seams of a dress, until finally, there was no hint that they had ever been separate.

"Whoa!" Cat grinned. "That's super-cool! How did you *do* that?"

"This is not how Reappearing Potion has worked before." Fizzbee picked up her vial and gave it a little shake. "Fizzbee is thinking that it may need to be mixed with water and used as a spray." She began muttering to herself, writing down complicated looking calculations on a notepad in front of her.

But Scooter wasn't listening. His heart was pounding at the sight of the words:

Here lies ye olde treasure of Captain DodgyBeard.

"Is this what I think it is?" He stared down at the map in front of him. "Because if it is, then that would mean – well, it would mean that there's *treasure under the jam factory!*"

"Scooter!" Fizzbee's head darted up from her calculations. "This is *exactly* what we are needing!"

Scooter grinned. Fizzbee was right. And treasure that was hundreds of years old had to be worth loads. Definitely enough to buy the factory back from Daffy at any rate! All he needed to do was to use this map and find it. Then maybe, just maybe, they could still get the factory back in time to host the Grand Reopening!

Except ... there was just one problem.

"Who was this Captain DodgyBeard?" Scooter pondered. "Because it sounds like he might have something to do with Daffy. And then, technically, wouldn't the treasure belong to her?"

"Maybe he was a pirate from a *really* long time ago?" Cat shrugged. "Daffy's great-great-grandad or something like that?"

"It figures that Daffy would have pirate ancestors." Scooter sighed as he looked back at the map. But it seemed that the Reappearing Potion hadn't finished its work yet. It continued to scribble and scrawl across the page, new words appearing before their eyes.

Ye Olde Tower of Dodgyness

Me treasure be buried somewhere secret
Whoever can find it, gets to keep-it
To help you enter, JAM is the key
But if you be faint-hearted, you better flee
For while jam is wonderful and jam is delicious
Down in my vaults jam can be vicious
Only if it be known to you how jam is made
Then you survive and treasure be paid
But if how to make the jam be unknown to you
Then down in my vaults, you findeth your doo-m

W

Here

olde

"Well, I guess that answers my question about who it belongs to! But *jam*?" He frowned. "What's DodgyBeard's treasure got to do with jam?" He read the poem again. The *'findeth your doom'* bit didn't sound great.

Mum and Dad might not like *that*.

But then, it also said that if you knew how to make jam, you'd survive. And if anyone knew how to make jam, it was Scooter! Plus, Mum *had* said that if Scooter found a stack of buried treasure, then they could buy back the factory. So, she'd *want* him to find DodgyBeard's treasure … right?

As Scooter's eyes lit up with hope, Cat stepped forwards.

"Before you get carried away – my Uncle Perry is already planning to find the treasure vaults during your Grand Reopening tonight. And then … he's planning to do something to

70

your factory. Something horrible." She gave a sharp shake of her head. "Uncle Perry's a rotten old crook. I came here to warn you!"

"But why?" Scooter cried. "We haven't done anything to him!"

"I don't understand it either. I mean, he does *really* hate jam. I'm not even sure why – he's never even tried it! It's completely weird. But I couldn't let him do anything to McLay's Jam!"

"It might not be McLay's Jam without that treasure." Scooter flopped onto a chair with a sigh. "If we don't find it by 6 p.m. tonight, then everyone will be here for the Grand Reopening of *Dodgy* Jam. Daffy Dodgy tricked us – the factory is hers, and the only way that'll change is if we buy it off her."

"Seriously?" Cat exclaimed. "You can't let her take your factory! Her doughnuts were the worst." She made a vomiting face.

71

"What is it with these grown-ups thinking it's OK to just nab our stuff? I mean, first Uncle Perry takes all of my parents' valuables, then he takes Mr Jammy, next he's planning to take the treasure. And now Daffy thinks it's OK to take your factory, too? We need to show them that they can't just—"

"Who is this Mr Jammy?" Fizzbee picked up a blueberry menacingly. "Another thief?"

"Oh no, it's OK!" Cat giggled. "Mr Jammy's my teddy. Uncle Perry stole him from my *actual bed.*"

"This Uncle Perry is verrrry bad." Fizzbee threw the blueberry to the floor.

"Anyway," Cat continued, "we'd better hurry if we're going to find that treasure. If we can get back before your Grand Reopening, then we can stop Daffy and Uncle Perry. It shouldn't be too tricky. All we need to do is to break into Dodgy Jam, find the entrance to the vaults, get through some booby traps and locate the treasure. Oh, and avoid *findeth-ing our doo-m*. All within ..." She looked at her watch and bit her lip. "... err, seven hours. Totally doable, right?"

Scooter smiled. He actually did have a solution to all of those challenges. But it meant showing Cat his inventions and Scooter wasn't entirely sure about that. She may have warned him about her uncle and brought them the map, but what if it was all just a trick so that she could steal his ideas, like Daffy?

"Scooter," Fizzbee whispered into his ear, as though she could read his exact thoughts.

"Fizzbee can see that Cat is not lying. Fizzbee is thinking that we can trust her."

"You can *see* it?" Scooter whispered. "Really?"

When Fizzbee first arrived at the jam factory, she had told Scooter that she could see creativity like a rainbow of colours around a person. It was actually why she'd landed on earth. The colours of Scooter's hyper-creativity were so bright that she'd seen them all the way from space! But Scooter didn't know that she could see honesty, too.

"When a person is lying, their creativity is red," Fizzbee explained. "People can be very creative when they are lying!" She stared hard at Cat again, then shook her head. "There is no red around Cat."

"So, shall we get going?" Cat pointed to the door. "I mean, if you want to get the treasure by 6 p.m. tonight, we'd better go right away, hadn't we?"

Scooter glanced down at his splint. There was no way he could go searching for treasure without making a plan and packing his supplies. Cat might be able to scale a factory wall and somersault down from a pipe, but Scooter would need a little help.

Luckily, he'd invented the perfect tools for that.

"I'll need to pack a few bits first." He whistled as two robotic hands extended down from the ceiling. "And I think we should have a bit of a plan. But yeah, OK. Let's find that treasure and get our factory back from Daffy!"

"Yes!" Cat punched the air in excitement as Fizzbee circled her head delightedly.

"Hand-Bots?" Scooter ordered. "We need to pack for a treasure hunt."

CHAPTER SIX

Perry Pincher and Colonel Pom Pom practised
doing the splits in the antiques store while Perry
ran over the plan for stealing the treasure.

"Of course at first, we'll have to make
it look like we're just attending the Grand
Reopening as guests like everyone else." Perry
stretched down over one leg. "But as soon as
we're inside, Colonel Pom Pom, you can use
your nose and sniff out the entrance to those
treasure vaults."

"**Meep.**" Colonel Pom Pom nodded from his perfect box splits position.

"I've got us a couple of loot bags each," Perry said, touching his nose to his toe. "So, we'll just take what we can." He hoisted himself stiffly out of the splits, stood up and stretched. "All we need to decide now is how we're going to sabotage that stinking factory. Ideally, I'd blow the whole place to smithereens. But perhaps we should just put some bricks in the machinery, or maybe we could even pour some superglue in the jam and bring the whole place to a standstill…"

"**Meep!**" Colonel Pom Pom sniggered delightedly.

"Let's head to the cellar and come up with a proper plan." Perry skipped down the stairs, flung the door open and leapt inside.

"Urgh!" He recoiled. There was a jam sandwich lying on the floor. "Get rid of it!"

He hid behind an old armchair as Colonel Pom Pom picked up the offending sandwich and flung it out of the door. "My dratted niece must have been in here. I can't think why she'd play such a rotten trick on me!" Perry flopped onto the armchair and rubbed his forehead wearily while Colonel Pom Pom massaged his temples.

Perry wriggled uncomfortably. There was something lumpy under his bottom.

He reached down and pulled out an old TV remote from under the cushion.

CLICK.

Perry jumped in surprise as Daffy's old television blinked to life.

He'd found it in a skip full of Daffy's old stuff when he'd been looking for the other half of the map. But it was broken. There was no sound and it only had one channel: something he'd never heard of called *Jam-Cam* that just showed a close-up of a suitcase with a warning sign on it.

Except ... he peered closer.

The suitcase was gone and now he could see inside a room. It was some kind of laboratory. There was a boy and—

"What's my *infernal niece* doing in there?" Perry sat bolt upright as he stared wide-eyed at the screen. She was talking to the boy and they were both leaning over a table looking at... "That's *MINE!*" He jumped up from the armchair, his eyes darting towards the back wall as he recognized his map on the screen in front of him. "And she's only gone and got both halves! Oh, that little toe rag! First, she leaves a jam sandwich in my loot room, then she nabs my map and now she's planning to *steal my treasure*! Next thing you know she'll be going up against us at the *One Owner and Their Pet Dance Championship*s!"

"Meep!" Colonel Pom Pom gave an indignant shimmy.

"You're so right." Perry smirked. "She wouldn't have a hope against *us*." He pointed the remote towards the TV and turned up the volume, just in time to hear the boy say:

"Let's find that treasure and get our factory back from Daffy!"

"Daffy?" Perry sat back down on the armchair and Colonel Pom Pom went back to massaging his temples. So Daffy was in charge of the factory again? Well, that made things a little easier. He smirked. He could easily charm his way past daft old Daffy Dodgy. He watched as Cat punched the air in excitement on the screen. She'd turned out to be a little sneakier than he'd thought. Perry's moustache twitched as a proud smile *almost*

crept onto his face. So, she was a chip off the old block after all!

Unfortunately for her, Perry Pincher wasn't easily out-sneaked.

"Change of plan, Colonel Pom Pom." He jumped up, grabbing an old clipboard from a shelf beside him. "We're getting into that factory right *now*."

"Right then." Scooter stood in front of a whiteboard as two robotic hands busied themselves beside him. One was packing a mechanical looking backpack with two jars of glow-in-the dark jam and enough jam sandwiches, blueberries and Brussels sprout Jam Slices (for Fizzbee) to feed them all for a month. The other was drawing a map of the Dodgy Jam factory on the whiteboard.

83

Cat watched them with fascination, her face a mixture of surprise and delight.

"These are my Hand-Bots," Scooter explained. "My hands can be a little stiff sometimes, so I developed the Hand-Bots to help me. Hand-Bots, this is Cat. She's going to be joining us on the treasure hunt." Scooter smiled as the two robotic hands stopped what they were doing and gave Cat a friendly wave.

"So, here's the plan," Scooter explained as Hand-Bot Two finished drawing the map. "I installed a rollercoaster into Dodgy Jam when we did it up. Daffy probably doesn't realize this, but it's connected to the rollercoaster in this factory, so that's our best way in." He watched as Hand-Bot Two drew a little cross on the map and started writing.

ROLLERCOASTER
ENTRY POINT

"Once we're inside, I'm pretty sure that the entrance to the vaults is here." Scooter pointed to a room labelled, *Inventions Gone Wrong Cupboard.* "Our biggest challenge is going to be getting from the Rollercoaster Entry Point to the cupboard without being seen by Daffy or Boris."

Hand-Bot Two drew a squiggly dotted line between the two *X*s followed by a picture of a stick figure lady and a guinea pig, labelled *Daffy* and *Boris*. "As soon as we're in that cupboard, we should be safe to look for the entrance to the vaults undisturbed."

"OK." Cat nodded. "What about finding the actual entrance? Have you got that figured out too?"

"*I* don't." Scooter shook his head, then grinned as Fizzbee hovered beside him, pulling out a small plant sprayer from behind her back with a wink. "But Fizzbee does. She's going to make sure we find the entrance, no problem."

"And…" Cat glanced down at Scooter's splint slightly awkwardly. "What about once we're inside? Are you going to be OK with the booby traps? Does your leg –" She pointed to his splint – "Well, does that make it trickier for you?"

Scooter followed Cat's gaze down to his left leg. It was true that cerebral palsy did make things a bit trickier sometimes, especially walking long distances. That was why he'd added a rollercoaster to the factory in the first place.

"It's never quite as easy away from the factory," he agreed. "But that's actually why I've developed a new invention. One that I can use *anywhere*." He tapped his backpack with a confident grin. "Just wait and see!"

"Scooter, this is flipping amazing!" Cat squealed as the rollercoaster whizzed through the factory, her grin growing wider with every loop as she stared at the spaghetti junction of pipes, pistons and pulleys below.

"Just wait until we get into Dodgy Jam!" Scooter beamed. "We made the rollercoaster even better in there!"

Tuck, tuck, tuck, tuck.

The little cart travelled slowly up towards the roof of the factory, through the skylight window and out into the blue sky outside.

Up, up and up the tracks continued, until finally they extended no further, bringing the little cart to a terrifying stop in mid-air, directly above the glass roof of the Dodgy Jam factory.

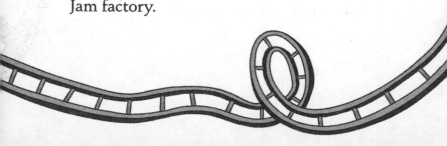

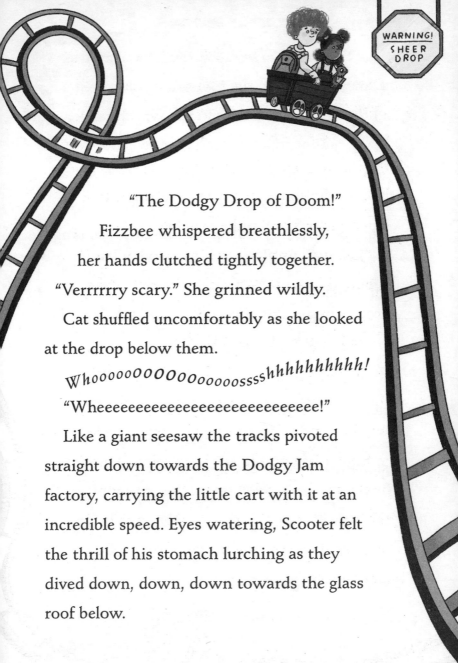

"The Dodgy Drop of Doom!"
Fizzbee whispered breathlessly,
her hands clutched tightly together.
"Verrrrrry scary." She grinned wildly.

Cat shuffled uncomfortably as she looked
at the drop below them.

Whoooooooooooooooooooossssshhhhhhhhhh!

"Wheeeeeeeeeeeeeeeeeeeeeeeeeeeeeeee!"

Like a giant seesaw the tracks pivoted
straight down towards the Dodgy Jam
factory, carrying the little cart with it at an
incredible speed. Eyes watering, Scooter felt
the thrill of his stomach lurching as they
dived down, down, down towards the glass
roof below.

"We're going to smash into the...!" Cat cried as a small window in the roof sprang open, just in time for the rollercoaster to whizz inside. They cannoned across the treetop canopy rope bridge, helter-skeltered down and—

"Shhhhhhhh! Everyone quiet!" Scooter slammed the *Stop* button on the cart, bringing it to a sudden halt with a jolt and an almighty

Phwwwwwsssssssssshhhhhhhh

"Errrr, Scooter?" Cat blinked twice, her hand held to her heart. "Why have we stopped upside down in a banana tree?"

Scooter pressed his finger to his lips and signalled towards the ground in reply.

Down below, Daffy was stomping across the factory floor, Boris in a baby carrier on her front. Scooter watched as she stopped a short way from the rollercoaster entry point, next to a bath full of jam, bubbles floating out of it.

She hesitated for a
moment, then, with a sly
grin, dipped her pointy
finger into the bath and licked it.

"She can't do that!" Scooter hissed. "She'll
contaminate the jam!"

"Hmm. Very nice, Boris. What do you think?"

He watched in horror as she did it again, this
time offering her finger to Boris to lick. "Urgh,
she's getting guinea pig spit in there now!"
Scooter wrinkled his nose as Daffy dipped her
finger into the bath a third time. "We'll have to
deep-clean the entire fac—" He gasped as she
picked up a jar of salt thoughtfully.

"But I think it needs a bit more salt." She
emptied the entire jar into the
bath, then took yet another dip.
"Ew." She gagged. "Maybe not."

Daffy offered some jam to Boris.

"Squeak." He wisely clamped his mouth shut with a firm shake of his head.

"Well, we're going to have to come up with some new inventions of our own, somehow, Boris," Daffy huffed as she trudged past the banana tree and towards the Jam Party Range.

Scooter pressed the *Start* button on the rollercoaster and the little group remained silent as the cart trundled quietly towards the factory floor.

"Let's just get to that cupboard as quickly as we can," Scooter muttered as they ducked and weaved their way past Daffy and Boris, rage bubbling inside him as he saw Daffy picking fruit from the strawberry wall and smacking one of the robotic hands as it tried to wrestle a strawberry back from her. "The quicker we get that treasure, the quicker we get Daffy out of *our* factory."

CHAPTER SEVEN

"I guess I was kind of expecting something
a bit more..." Cat stood in the centre of the
Inventions Gone Wrong cupboard, by a wall
of Jam Toilet Rolls. "... *treasure-y?* Are you sure

the entrance to the vaults is in here? I can't see anything to do with this pirate, Captain DodgyBeard. He could at least have a Jolly Roger up somewhere, or better still a cutlass!"

"I'm sure this is the right place." Scooter studied the map for the millionth time as Fizzbee landed on a shelf beside him and

opened her backpack. "This has to be it." He gave the cupboard a dubious look.

It was filled with shelves of carefully labelled inventions. All the

things he'd tried over the last few months that had gone a bit wrong.

He hadn't realized there were

quite so many.

HIGHLY EXPLOSIVE
(on contact with water)

"So…" Cat held up a Jam Toilet Roll as Fizzbee reached for her backpack. "What *exactly* were you thinking when you came up with *this*?"

"I just thought that jam smells nice and maybe a jammy toilet roll would make the toilet smell nice too." Scooter shrugged.

Cat thought about it.

"That actually makes sense. So, what went wrong?"

"As soon as it got wet, it became really sticky and completely blocked the toilet … not to mention most of the factory plumbing. It took Mum weeks to get it all working again." He rubbed the back of his neck. "My inventions don't *always* go right."

"But Scooter, no inventions are perfect right away." Fizzbee pulled out a little spray bottle from her backpack. "Sometimes they need lots of work." She began methodically

spraying the walls of the cupboard. "And sometimes, they can be used for something else. We did not know that Reappearing Potion would be so good at finding treasure!" She grinned. "Maybe Fizzbee will rename Reappearing Potion and call it Treasure-finding Potion!"

THUD, THUD, THUD, THUD.

The little group hushed as they heard heavy footsteps approaching.

"Ooh, Boris! Look at this cupboard!" They all turned towards the voice coming from outside the door. "Inventions Gone Wrong? I won't need to come up with any new ideas if I can fix one of these and palm it off as my own!"

"Quick!" Scooter hissed. "It's Daffy! Get behind the Jam Toilet Rolls!" They dived down just as the door opened and a long shadow filled the room.

"Did you hear something, Boris?" Daffy stared suspiciously into the cupboard.

"**Squeak**." Boris shrugged from the baby carrier as Daffy began rifling through the shelves. She stopped as her eyes fell on the wall of Jam Toilet Rolls.

"Ooooh, Boris, what a fantastic idea! That really would make the toilet smell lovely."

Boris rolled his eyes as Daffy reached towards a Jam Toilet Roll, just millimetres from Scooter's head. "Well, I'll just take a couple."

DING DONG.

She stopped, the tips of her fingers almost brushing the top of Scooter's hair as she turned towards the front door.

"Was that the door?"

DING DONG.

Rat-a-tat-tat.

"All right, all right. I'm coming," Daffy muttered. She picked up a jar of Popping Candy Jam, looked at it thoughtfully, then stomped out of the cupboard and shut the door behind her.

Perry waited outside the front door of the jam factory, his most charming smile plastered on his face, an important looking clipboard under his arm and Colonel Pom Pom peeking out from his inside pocket. "As soon as she opens the door, Colonel Pom Pom, you climb down and start sniffing out the entrance to those vaults. Leave me to deal with Daffy Dodgy." He smirked.

"What d'ya want?" Daffy opened the front door. She had a fat white guinea pig in a baby carrier on her front and held a jar of disgusting looking jam. "If you're here collecting for anything, then you should know that I'm armed and dangerous. So, I suggest that you just shove right..."

"Good day, ma chérie." Perry interrupted her with a winsome wink, the gold of his tooth glinting as he leant casually in the doorway.

Daffy hesitated, the jar of Popping Candy Jam lowering just a little.

Perry gave his moustache a villainous little twizzle.

"Oooh." Daffy giggled. "You charmer." She put the jar of jam down on the floor beside her as Colonel Pom Pom poked his head out from Perry's inside pocket and prepared to sneak into the factory.

"**Squeak**." Boris eyed him suspiciously.

"**Meep.**" Colonel Pom Pom withdrew back into Perry's pocket.

100

"I'm here because I am looking for some brats," Perry continued. "I mean *rats*." He held up his clipboard.

"Rats?" Daffy frowned as Boris ducked down into the carrier, just a little, his eyes still watching Perry's pocket suspiciously.

"Oh yes." Perry pretended to pick a piece of fluff from his velvet jacket. "You can't have a Grand Reopening if you've got *any* rodents in here."

"Well, no. Of course not, Officer." Daffy crossed her arms protectively over the baby carrier. "But I can assure you, we don't have *any* rats here."

"I'm sure." Perry took a step forwards. "I'll just need to case the joint quickly. I mean, inspect this establishment." He gave her his most charming smile and waggled his eyebrows attractively. "Just to be certain."

"Have you got something in your eye, Officer?" Daffy stood firmly in the doorway. "And I don't think you're allowed to check for rats without some kind of warrant."

Perry sighed. This wasn't proving to be as easy as he'd imagined. It was time to give Daffy the full charm offensive.

"Oh, dear lady." He got down on one knee, reached for Daffy's hand and lifted it to his lips. "You should go to prison."

"Prison?" Daffy took a step back. "But I haven't done anything!"

"Because..." Perry stood up, held her in his arms and looked down into her eyes. "You've stolen my heart."

"Oh my!" Daffy blushed as Perry began
to lead her around the room in a foxtrot,
forgetting that Colonel Pom Pom, in his inside
pocket, was now nose-to-nose with a very
disgruntled looking Boris.

They danced one way. Then the other.
Twirling and swirling around the jam factory,
until they were directly outside the Inventions
Gone Wrong cupboard.

INVENTIONS
GONE WRONG
CUPBOARD

"Has anyone found anything yet?" Scooter whispered, as back inside the cupboard the little team frantically scanned the walls for any sign of Captain DodgyBeard's treasure.

"We need to get out of here." Cat cast the door a nervous glance as Fizzbee gave the Reappearing Potion spray a frustrated little shake. "Daffy might be back any second!"

One lone drop of Reappearing Potion fell to the floor.

"Scooter, look!" Fizzbee pointed down.

Where the drop had fallen, a flourishing letter J had appeared on the tile beneath his left foot.

"The floor!" Scooter gasped as Cat gripped his arm in excitement. "We didn't think of that! Quick as you can, Fizz! Spray the whole thing!" They watched, their breath held in anticipation as Fizzbee showered the floor with Reappearing Potion.

Two more letters appeared.

"MAJ?" Fizzbee rubbed her chin. "What word is this?"

"It's JAM!" Scooter hit his forehead with his palm. "Of course! The map even said that jam is the key! We must have to spell it out. Quickly, let's each stand on a letter!"

Scooter remained on the J.

Cat leapt onto the A.

Fizzbee hovered down towards the M, just as the door to the cupboard was flung open.

They froze like statues as outside a man with a moustache and a peg on his nose twirled Daffy on the spot, then kissed her hand.

"Urgh." Cat gagged.

"Thank you, my dear. That was magical." Perry and Daffy's eyes locked in a weird mushy sort of way, before he spun her into the cupboard, straight onto the letter M, then neatly slammed the door in her face.

RUUUUUUUMMMMMMMMBBBLLLEEEE.

"Errrr. What was that?" Daffy turned slowly around, and her eyes rested on Scooter, Fizzbee and Cat. "Oi! What are *you* doing in here?"

SLAM.

An iron gate dropped from above, sealing the room behind it.

SLAM. SLAM. SLAM.

Three more iron gates followed,
surrounding them like a cage.

"Squeak?" Boris asked nervously
from the baby carrier.

Whoooooooooosssssshhhhh.

"Arrrrrgggggggghhhhhhhhhhhhhh!"

Cold, damp air rushed past as the
tiny cage fell down, down, down
into a black pit below.

CHAPTER EIGHT

"Quickly, Colonel Pom Pom," Perry hissed as he turned the key in the lock of the Inventions Gone Wrong cupboard. "Now she's out of the way, you can sniff out that treasure."

He heard a faint scream from inside the cupboard.

"Oh dear." He sighed. "She really fell for me."

"**Meep.**" Colonel Pom Pom peeked out from Perry's inside pocket and scuttled down to the floor. He licked his paws and smoothed down his whiskers, then gave the room a cautious sniff.

Zing!

His fluffy tail bolted as if it had been struck by electricity.

"That's it, Colonel Pom Pom!" Perry clicked his heels delightedly. "You've got the scent!" Colonel Pom Pom put his nose to the ground and began sniffling and snaffling his way around the factory. First one way. Then the other.

He gave the Inventions Gone Wrong cupboard a good snuffle.

Then shook his head.

Next, he turned back towards the old wishing well in the centre of the factory.

He stopped, climbed onto the ledge, took a long sniff and pointed into the well.

"Down there?" Perry peered down the well.

"**Meep.**" Colonel Pom Pom nodded.

"All right." Perry pulled a bucket on a rope out of the well. "Let's go." He stopped as he noticed the jar of Popping Candy Jam on the floor, then picked it up and pocketed it with a sly grin. "We never did decide how to sabotage this place, did we?"

Scooter felt his insides lurch as the tiny room fell into the cold darkness below.

"Ar͞rrrgggggggghhhhhhhhhhhhhhh!" Daffy screamed.

"Sqeeeeaaaaaaaaaaaaaakkkkkkkkkkkkkk!" Boris squeaked.

"We need to slow our fall!" Scooter cried as down, down, and down again they plummeted.

Daffy stopped screaming to take a breath.

"Or we will be squished like bugs!" Fizzbee shouted.

The screaming began again.

"Have you got any inventions that can help?" Cat bellowed. "Maybe even some earplugs?" She glared at Daffy pointedly.

Scooter looked around the little cage desperately, his eyes falling on some packets of Jam Bubble Gum scattered on the floor. Wait a minute! His face lit up. The Jam Bubble Gum that made floating bubbles!

As if she could read his mind, Fizzbee darted towards them.

"Everyone, chew for your lives!"

Fizzbee passed the gum around, until everyone was frantically chewing and blowing bubble gum bubbles. Bubbles floated into the air as the lift continued plummeting down, little by little slowing their fall.

THWUMP

They landed. There was a short *ding* and a rumbling sound as the iron gate slid open in front of them.

"I can't see anything!"

"Gerroffffff me."

"Where are we?"

"Squeak."

Scooter blinked. It was pitch black down here. A small orange orb began to shine softly beside him. He turned towards the light, gasping as he realized that it was Fizzbee. Her tiny body was glowing from within, dimly lighting the room and revealing a long, stone passageway ahead.

Huge cobwebs hung down from the ceiling and a thick pile of dust covered the floor. A cold, musty draught wafted towards them. The air smelled like an old book that hadn't been opened for a hundred years. But there was another smell too. Something sweet and familiar.

"Now *this* is more like it!" Cat grinned.

"We must be miles below the factory." Scooter looked up at the long, dark shaft above them.

"Where have you taken me?" Daffy peered out at the passageway. *"Take me back!"* She stamped her foot. "You can't just come into my factory and kidnap me! It's exactly the kind of low-down rotten trick that I'd expect from … well, me," she finished.

"Squeak." Boris agreed.

"I demand that you return me to my factory right now!" Daffy pulled a Jam Toilet Roll off her head, gave it a furtive glance, then stuffed it into the baby carrier with Boris.

"Believe me. We don't want you here. And we're definitely not *kidnapping* you." Scooter rolled his eyes. "You can go back up in that lift right— Oh." He looked towards the lift, just in time to see it float out of reach and back up to the surface without them.

"Scooter." Fizzbee pulled him aside, casting a furtive glance towards Daffy and Boris. "This is not part of the planning."

"I know," Scooter muttered as Cat joined the huddle. "Daffy always ruins everything."

"Well, we have to get rid of her before we go looking for treasure!" Cat raised her eyebrows.

"What are you talking about over there? Did someone say *treasure*?" Daffy's eyes narrowed, then her face filled with a sudden understanding. "Oh my giddy aunt, this must be the entrance to Great

Grandpa DodgyBeard's treasure vaults!" She began hopping from one foot to the other in excitement. "Nobody's ever found it before. I didn't even think it was real! But … well, I've found it now, haven't I! Oh Boris, we're going to be millionaires!" she squealed. "Millionaire owners of the most wonderful jam factory in the world! My dreams are all coming true at once!"

"Hold on just a minute!" Scooter stepped forwards. "You didn't find anything! We're the ones that found the entrance. And we're the ones with the map to the treasure."

"Who cares if you've got the map? Fact is, it's *my* treasure." Daffy gave the map a quick glance. "It's in the name, isn't it? Captain *DodgyBeard*." She rolled her eyes.

"Actually, it belongs to whoever finds it first." Scooter held up the map as Fizzbee pointed to the poem. "It says it right here:

> **Me treasure be buried somewhere secret**
> **Whoever can find it, gets to keep-it.**

And seeing as we've got the map, I guess that's going to be us."

"Scooter," Fizzbee whispered. "Fizzbee is thinking that we can make a deal." She turned towards Daffy. "If we help you find the treasure, will Daffy give Scooter back the factory?"

Daffy didn't answer right away. She seemed to be thinking it over very hard.

"Squeak." Boris nudged her with a little nod.

"Fine." She sighed dramatically. "But if you don't find it before the Grand Reopening tonight, then the deal's off and everyone will celebrate the opening of Dodgy Jam."

"You've got a deal." Scooter looked at his watch. "It's a truce until 6 p.m. tonight. That gives us four hours, so we'd better get going right away." He took off his backpack, lay it on the floor, pressed a large orange button on the front of it and backed away.

The little backpack shuddered and stuttered, folded and flipped, until it was

a gleaming orange *quad bike*, the word RALPH
emblazoned across it on a strip of painted fire.

"Whoa!" Cat grinned. "That's amazing!"

"I've got to hand it to you, you're a worthy
arch nemesis, Scooter McLay." Daffy looked
impressed as she stared down at the control
panel.

"This is my Robotic Air Laboratory and
Portable Hovercraft." Scooter sat astride the
quad bike. "Or RALPH, as I like to call him."
He grinned as a small hand extended from the
back of it, placed a bicycle helmet on his head,
strapped on a seat belt and gave him a friendly
thumbs up. "Thanks, Hand-Bot Three." Scooter
smiled as the hand folded back into the bike
and Fizzbee landed in what looked like a cup
holder, but was actually a jam tart holder.

"Hey, RALPH." Cat smiled warmly as she climbed onboard.

"Actually, I think I should be the one to ride on that." Daffy blocked their path, her hands on her hips. "After all, I'm 78 so *I'm* the oldest and that means *I* get to go on the quad bike. It's how these things work. I get to choose who I ride with, too. And I choose Boris."

"78?" Fizzbee nodded thoughtfully. "Then Fizzbee is thinking that Daffy is not the oldest here. On Fizzbee's planet, we age much more slowly than humans. In human years, Fizzbee is 83." She gave Scooter a cheeky wink. "And Fizzbee chooses to ride with Scooter and Cat."

"What?" Daffy spluttered.

"Shall we go, then?" Scooter smiled smugly as he pressed the *Hover Power* button.

With a gentle jolt, RALPH's wheels raised slightly from the ground, before turning horizontally and hovering above the floor.

"No." Daffy stamped her foot. "That's cheating, that's not…"

THUD.

"Err." She lifted her foot. "I think I may have stepped on some kind of button just here."

RUUUUUUUUMMMMMMMMBBBLLLEEEE.

An ominous rumbling sound filled the passageway.

"What was that?" Scooter stared down at the floor, which began to creak and groan, as if a giant mechanical beast was slowly waking up below them. It shuddered and bounced and started moving like a conveyor belt, carrying a disgruntled looking Daffy with it.

"Booby traps, I'd say." Cat raised her eyebrows with a knowing nod. "Probably something really nasty up there."

"What do you mean something nasty?" Daffy peered ahead nervously as the conveyor belt began to pick up speed, carrying her further into the tunnel. Scooter followed cautiously behind on RALPH. "I can't see *anything*. Well, nothing other than a couple of statues of – awwwwww! They're statues of guinea pigs and they're so cu— ARRRRGGGGGGHHHHHHHHH!" Daffy turned on her heel and began legging it back towards them. "They're *pirate* guinea pig statues and they're trying to murder me!"

"Squeeeaaaaak!" Boris nodded in terror from the baby carrier.

"Pirate guinea pig statues?" Scooter peered forwards sceptically. He could make out the statues ahead on either side of the tunnel. They stood on their hind legs, their paws out in front of them like little begging dogs. Except, in their tiny guinea pig paws, they held *giant* cutlasses.

Giant cutlasses that were now swooshing up and down, slicing anything in their way.

"Help!" Daffy cried, her legs picking up

speed as the conveyor belt grew ever faster.

Whoooosh. Thud. Whoooosh. Thud. Whoooosh. Thud.

Daffy fell forwards, quickly scrambling to her knees. "Save yourself, Boris!" She untied the baby carrier. "You can outrun them. I'm done for!" Boris took one look at the lethal cutlasses ahead, then bolted towards the safety of RALPH. "Oi!" Daffy momentarily forgot her impending doom. "You're seriously going to leave me?"

Scooter met Fizzbee's eyes as she hovered out of the jam tart holder. She gave him a grim nod, then darted towards Daffy.

"How are we going to get past those statues, Scooter?" Cat asked from behind him, her voice wild with excitement.

Scooter watched the slicing, chopping action of the cutlasses as Fizzbee dived bravely towards Daffy. There was a short pause in between each swoosh of the cutlass. It was probably only a second or two but if they were fast enough, they could make it through. He'd have to time it just right.

Up ahead, Daffy watched as the statues grew ever closer, the back of her hand pressed dramatically to her forehead. "Goodbye, cruel world," she whispered as she closed her eyes and waited for...

"Waaaahh! Whadddya doing?" She turned as Fizzbee landed on her upturned bum and

hoisted her into the air by her brown velour
trousers, heaving her unsteadily towards
RALPH. Daffy grabbed a panting Boris as
Fizzbee deposited them on the handlebars, just
as the cutlasses rose back up.

"Hold tight, everyone!" Scooter cried as he
pressed the *Super Speed* button.

Scooter felt his breath squeezed out of him as RALPH catapulted forwards like a bullet.

Daffy and Boris were thrown headfirst into Scooter's lap as Fizzbee clung to the jam tart holder for dear life. Cat hollered and whooped as if this were the best rollercoaster ride of her life as the little quad bike hurtled along. Past the deadly statues and on through the dark, dusty passageways in a blur of speed, the air growing colder with every passing moment.

Scooter pressed the *STOP* button and let out a sigh of relief as RALPH came to a gentle halt, just as the passageway opened up into a round, high-ceilinged cavern.

For a moment the little group did nothing but breathe.

"That was incredible!" Cat jumped down from RALPH. She hesitated for a moment as she looked around the cavern, her nose scrunching in confusion at another cluster of statues lining the walls.

"What is it with all these statues of guinea pigs? Do you think these ones are going to try and chop us to pieces too?"

"I'm alive!" Daffy rolled awkwardly out and onto her back. She panted and stared up at Scooter, then over to Fizzbee, now hovering up from the jam tart holder. "You saved me."

She gave Fizzbee a small grateful smile, before turning to Boris, her face hardening. "And *you* left me."

"**Squeak**." Boris looked a little shamefaced.

"It's all right." Daffy's face softened. "You know I can't stay angry at you." She noticed the statues surrounding them. "Argh!" She leapt up with her arms in front of her but relaxed as she noticed that none of them were holding cutlasses. In fact, they were all in regal looking poses, names written beneath each of them. "Oh look, Boris! These are your ancestors."

"But why are there statues of Boris' ancestors down here?" Cat frowned. "Jam and guinea pigs? This is the weirdest pirate *ever*!"

"Oh, don't underestimate Great Grandpa DodgyBeard. He was the most fearsome pirate ever known!" Daffy began studying the guinea pig statues. "Every Dodgy in history has had a guinea pig companion, you know." She bent down and scratched behind Boris' ear. "Great Grandpa DodgyBeard's guinea pig was Deadly Doris. He loved her so much that he even made a statue of her out of pure gold. It's probably down here somewhere. Guinea pigs are a Dodgy's best friend."

Daffy watched as Boris deposited a little poo pellet on the floor beside her and gave a wistful sigh. "And as for jam, well let's just say he loved it. Started out as a way to stop the scurvy, but it became more to him than that."

"Scooter." Fizzbee hovered by his shoulder.

"Look!" She pointed to three huge stone, cobwebbed passages on the other side of the cavern. Each one had a different word chiselled into the stonework.

BOILING

CHOPPING

BOTTLIN

"It must be something to do with that poem on the map." Scooter slid down from RALPH and began handing out glow-in-the-dark jam lanterns. "Remember what it said? *If it be known to you how jam is made, Then you survive, and treasure be paid.* That's got to be a clue." He looked at the chiselled words again. The first part of making jam was to chop the fruit, so maybe they should go through the CHOPPING entrance.

Except... He looked behind him. They'd already been chopped, hadn't they? The next part of the process was to add sugar. But there didn't seem to be a doorway with the word SUGAR above it.

"I don't think we should go through any of those doorways." Scooter stepped back cautiously. "There must be another entrance."

Scooter, Fizzbee and Cat began searching the room as Daffy and Boris continued to study the statues.

"Well, old Grandpa DodgyBeard got that wrong!" Daffy pointed to one of the statues. "Boris never had an ancestor called S. Ugar! It doesn't even have the usual *-oris* rhyme! And the ear is wonky too." She tried to straighten it.

RUUUUUUUMMMMMMMMBBBBLLLEEEE.

"Ooopsie." Daffy stepped back nervously. "I think I might have done something again."

"ARGH!" Cat screamed as the floor gave way beneath her and she tumbled out of sight.

"Cat!" Scooter cried. "Are you OK?" He peered over the ledge. It was dark, except for the small green light of Cat's glow-in-the-dark jam lantern.

"I'm all right!" Cat called up. "I'm in…" There was

132

a pause. "I dunno. I think it's some kind of funnel? There's a hole beneath me. But luckily for me it's been blocked. And…" There was a pause. "Well, there's sand everywhere. I guess that's what's blocked it."

"Sand?" Scooter called down. "Can you, er, maybe eat some?"

"You want me to eat *sand*?" Cat retorted doubtfully.

"Well, yes, if you wouldn't mind?" Scooter replied.

There was a short pause, before…

"Scooter, it's not sand, it's sugar!"

"Yes!" Scooter punched the air. "I knew sugar was next. That must be the way to go!"

He turned to Fizzbee. "Can you have a little look for me please, Fizz, and see why Cat didn't get through?"

Scooter watched as Fizzbee's orange glow hovered down over the ledge, drifted towards the green of Cat's lantern and went dark for a moment, before reappearing a few seconds later.

"Scooter!" Fizzbee grinned as she returned. "It is a funnel! Fizzbee went inside. It leads to a river and a little boat. Except..." She paused. "It has been blocked by old sugar. The hole is only just big enough for Fizzbee to fly through." She peered at Boris. "And maybe Boris, too."

"**Squeak**." Boris shook his head, turned his bum towards them and deposited a little poo pellet.

"I don't think Boris wants to go down there." Daffy crossed her arms, her eyebrows raised. "And anyway, even

134

if he could get through the funnel, how are you going to get the rest of us out? Unless your fancy quad bike can blast it?"

"Actually..." Fizzbee landed on RALPH, reached down into the jam tart holder and heaved out her little suitcase of inventions. "Fizzbee has something that could help." She opened it and pulled out a jar of jam.

"Fizzbee!" Scooter exclaimed. "You brought your inventions?"

"Yes, Scooter." Fizzbee nodded shyly. "When Reappearing Potion proved useful, Fizzbee thought that maybe her other inventions might be useful too. So, Fizzbee brought them with her. In case of emergency."

Scooter peered over the ledge, then back to the jar in Fizzbee's hand. Was eating Shrinking

Strawberry Jam really a good idea? It wouldn't be the first time he'd tried it. But it had taken quite a long time to get him back to full size last time. That was actually the whole reason why his parents had banned all of Fizzbee's inventions in the first place.

"Fizzbee has adjusted the recipe since the last time you used it." Fizzbee seemed to read his mind. "One teaspoon and you will only stay small for five minutes."

"You adjusted the recipe?" Scooter couldn't help asking.

"Yes, Scooter." Fizzbee looked down at her little feet. "Fizzbee wanted to make her invention right." She paused, then gave a small, sad smile. "Even if it could never be used."

"I'm sorry, Fizz." Scooter put his hand out for Fizzbee and she toddled past his fingers onto his palm.

All of a sudden, it didn't seem quite fair that

Fizzbee wasn't allowed to use her inventions. Scooter wasn't sure how he'd feel if his parents had banned him from doing the same. There'd be no jam factory for a start. But it would make him unhappy, too, and Scooter couldn't bear to think of Fizzbee unhappy. All she ever did was try to help him. "I should have stuck up for you when Mum and Dad said that your inventions were banned."

"It is OK, Scooter." Fizzbee hugged his thumb. "It is not the first time Fizzbee has been banned from using inventions." She giggled sheepishly.

"So, what else did you bring?" Scooter couldn't help asking as Fizzbee opened the suitcase to reveal her inventions. There were all of her vials and test tubes and even the small shaker of glittering Friendship Sprinkles.

"NO, BORIS!" she cried as Boris pounced on the shaker and emptied the entire pot into his mouth in seconds. "This is Fizzbee's Friendship Sprinkles!"

"What did you do to my little Boris?" Daffy scooped up the guinea pig and pulled him into her arms protectively.

"He will be OK," Fizzbee explained.
"Friendship Sprinkles just make friendships
much stronger. So long as Boris already likes
you a little bit…"

They all turned towards Boris as he
looked up at each of them, a woozy smile
on his little face.

First, he looked at Scooter.

He blinked and shook his head.

He turned to Fizzbee.

Then shook his head again.

He peered down the hole towards Cat,
shrugged and turned to Daffy, their eyes
finally meeting.

"Yes, Boris, it's me." Daffy
spoke softly. "Your best fr—"

"**Squeak**." Boris gazed at
her and released a little
heart-shaped poo pellet into
the crook of Daffy's arm.

"Oh Boris." Daffy hugged him tight. "You've never shown me you care before."

"It looks like the only way to find DodgyBeard's treasure is if we eat some of Fizzbee's Shrinking Strawberry Jam and get through that blocked funnel." Scooter got back to the business in hand. "Well, us humans anyway. Fizzbee and Boris are fine to get through."

"Sounds good to me!" Cat's voice drifted up from below.

Scooter watched as Fizzbee hovered down towards Cat with a spoonful of Shrinking Strawberry Jam, then pressed the *Stealth Mode*

button on RALPH. The little quad bike folded
and flipped into a small backpack again. Scooter
picked it up and heaved it onto his shoulder.

"Except, I'm NOT eating that," Daffy
declared as Fizzbee returned with an empty
spoon. "And there's nothing that you can do
to persuade…"

SWOoOOOOoooOOOOSH.
"Argh!"

They ducked just in time as a volley of
arrows hurtled out of the guinea pig statues
towards them.

"Seriously?" Daffy sighed. "Fine." She took
a spoonful from Fizzbee. "Let's just get out of
here."

CHAPTER TEN

"Woohooooo!" Scooter cried in delight as he
and Fizzbee zipped down through a tunnel of
crystallized sugar on her jam tart.

Swoooooosh.

They soared into a large smooth stone
grotto, a huge pile of soft sugar below.

"Yee-ha!" Daffy giggled from her position
astride Boris as they whizzed out from the funnel,
landing with a soft flump on the pile of sugar.

"Wheeeeeeeeeeee!" Cat beamed as she
landed with a muffled thump beside them.

"That was amazing, Fizzbee!" Scooter grinned as Fizzbee brought down the jam tart a short distance away, allowing Scooter to step out just as he began to feel a tingling sensation and—

POP.

He blinked.

He was back to his normal size.

He turned towards Cat and Daffy as they too popped back to size.

"Thank you, Boris." Daffy picked up Boris and placed him carefully back into the baby carrier.

"Squeak." Boris nuzzled into her adoringly.

"Fizz, that's so clever!" Scooter checked his watch and gave her a high-five. "Five minutes exactly!"

"Thank you, Scooter." Fizzbee blushed.

The little group brushed themselves down as they peered around the grotto.

Sugar stalactites hung from the ceiling like beautiful crystals overhead. A small tunnel marked the way forwards and from inside came the sound of lapping water.

"The next stage of making jam is to add water." Scooter lay his backpack on the floor again. "So, I'm pretty sure that we should head down there." He pressed the large orange button on the front of it and backed away.

Shhhhhh takka takkka whiiiirrrrrrrrrrr SCCCHHPLOP.

The little backpack shuddered and stuttered and … fell quiet.

He pressed it again.

Whirrrrrrr. CRUNCCCCHHHH.

A pile of sugar sprinkled to the floor from inside the backpack.

"Uh-oh!" Scooter frowned as Hand-Bot Three creaked out from inside the backpack holding a small pile of sugar in the palm of its hand. It sprinkled it to the floor, then gave Scooter a stiff thumbs down. "The mechanisms must have got clogged up with sugar."

"Hey, Scooter, it's OK!" Cat called from up ahead. "You won't need RALPH just now anyway. We can use this boat."

Scooter picked up RALPH, heaved the backpack onto his shoulder and joined Cat. She was standing at the edge of a small underground stream. Water lapped onto the pathway and a wooden boat was tied to an old iron ring. Scooter followed the stream with his eyes as it snaked into the dark passageway ahead.

"Come on then." He took a deep breath and stepped carefully into the boat as Cat held it steady. "Let's see what old DodgyBeard has in store for us next."

Back in the factory, Perry clicked his fingers at the edge of the wishing well while Colonel Pom Pom bopped his head up and down in time with the beat.

"And a one, and a two, and a one, two, three."

Perry leapt across, raised his legs up into mid-air box splits, then landed perfectly, bum first, in the tiny tin bucket of the old wishing well, his gangly limbs spilling over the sides. Colonel Pom Pom star-jumped gleefully onto his lap.

"That was perfect!" Perry cried. "We should use that in the *One Owner and Their Pet Dance Championships*. We'll call it ... *The Bucket Bum Landing*. The judges will go wild for it!" He peered down nervously at the black hole beneath them. "You're sure the treasure is down there, Colonel Pom Pom?"

"**Meep.**" Colonel Pom Pom pointed downwards with a quick sniff and a firm nod.

"I wonder if there'll be any booby traps?" Perry wondered out loud as he began winching them down into the dark well-shaft.

"**Meep.**" Colonel Pom Pom flexed his muscles.

"You're so right, Colonel Pom Pom." Perry gave a sly grin. "No booby traps could get the better of us!"

As they got lower and lower, Perry couldn't help noticing that the walls were lined with a sticky coating of some kind. He reached out a finger to touch it and took a hesitant sniff.

147

"Ewwwwwww! Colonel Pom Pom! It's *jam*!" He straightened the peg on the end of his nose as he looked around wildly. "We're surrounded!"

"**Meewwwwwp.**" Colonel Pom Pom let out a meep of disgust.

"Quick, let's get down there fast!" Perry gagged. "Before I'm sick." He continued winching frantically.

Drip.

A tiny drop of jam glooped onto the edge of his moustache.

"AAAARRRRRR-
GGGGGGGHHHHH
HHHHHHHHH-
HHHHHH!" Perry
screamed in terror,
sweating now.

"Colonel Pom Pom!
Get it off! Get it off!"

Colonel Pom Pom opened his bum bag, pulled out a pair of scissors and cut one side of Perry's moustache right off, throwing it over the edge of the bucket as if it was a grenade about to explode.

Perry watched in shock as it fell below them.

"My beautiful moustache!" He grabbed at what was left of it, trying to give the tiny tuft a villainous twizzle and completely forgetting that in doing so, he'd let go of the rope for the bucket. He paused, meeting Colonel Pom Pom's eyes. They both turned towards the rope.

Whooooooooooossshhhhhh.

"AAAARRRRRRGGGGGGGHHHHH HHHHHHHHHHHHHHHH."

"MEEEEEEEEEEEEEEEEEPPP PPPPPPPPPPPP."

Down, down, down they fell into the black hole below.

"So, what is it with all the jam references?" Cat asked Daffy as the boat meandered slowly along the underground river. "Why was it so important to Captain DodgyBeard?"

"Yes!" Scooter nodded. "I've been wondering that too."

"Well, if you knew anything about anything, then you'd know that jam turned Great Grandpa DodgyBeard's life around." Daffy raised her eyebrows haughtily. "He might have started out as the most fearsome pirate ever known, but jam changed all that. He loved it almost as much as he loved his guinea pig, Deadly Doris. He gave up his pirating life and spent all his time trying to find the perfect jam recipe. Apparently, he did. Not that anyone ever found it."

"Really?" Scooter turned to her in surprise.

"Yes, actually." Daffy nodded proudly. "In

fact, I come from a long line of jam makers.
Since Great Grandpa DodgyBeard, every
Dodgy has continued the tradition. That is
until me, anyway." She sighed as she pulled out
a notebook from her pocket and opened it up
for them to see.

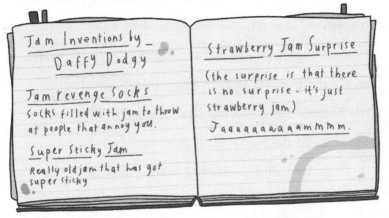

Jam Inventions by
    Daffy Dodgy

Jam revenge Socks
Socks filled with jam to throw
at people that annoy you.

Super Sticky Jam
Really old jam that has got
super sticky

Strawberry Jam Surprise

(the surprise is that there
is no surprise - it's just
strawberry jam)

Jaaaaaaaaaammmm.

"You see? My ideas are terrible." Daffy
threw the book down to the floor.

"Sometimes rubbish things can get better."
Fizzbee hovered down, picked up Daffy's
notebook and handed it back to her. "Fizzbee's
Shrinking Strawberry Jam was terrible at first!"
She smiled kindly.

"But I'm useless." Daffy shoved the book back in her pocket. "I wouldn't even know where to start."

"Well, when I come up with a new idea, I start by thinking about a problem I have. Something I want to solve." Scooter opened his backpack and smiled as Hand-Bot Three stiffly passed him the jam sandwiches and blueberries that he'd packed before they left. "And then I think about the properties of jam and how it could help me solve that problem."

"I'm listening..." Daffy leant forwards, her chin resting on the back of her hand.

"Like my first invention." Scooter lifted one of the sandwiches. "The Jam Slice. I came up with that because I don't find it easy to hold my knife to spread jam ... and I didn't want my mum always making my jam sandwiches. So, I thought, how could I develop something to help me make my jam sandwich ... and hey presto! The Jam Slice!" He smiled as Fizzbee landed on his shoulder. Cat was listening now too.

"And take my jam bubble bath." Scooter was quite enjoying this. "Well, that came about because I was hungry in the bath and I thought, wouldn't it be nice if I could just have a jam snack right here? Hey presto! Banana Jam Bubble Bath, containing tiny jam bubble pearls!" He grinned. "So, maybe start by thinking about a problem that you want to solve and then see how jam could fix it?"

"Well..." Daffy thought for a moment. "I'm a bit hungry."

"OK…" Scooter passed her a jam sandwich. There was plenty for everyone.

"And I'd quite like a nice biscuit right now." Daffy passed the sandwich to Boris.

"OK…" Scooter watched as Boris took a little nibble of sandwich. "So, how could jam fix that?"

Daffy thought hard for a moment.

"Scooter!" Fizzbee stared around Daffy's head in awe. "Fizzbee can see that Daffy is having an idea! Fizzbee can see colours!"

"Well, maybe I could invent a biscuit with jam in it."

"A verrrry little bit of colour," Fizzbee elaborated. But Daffy was getting excited now.

"You know what?" She hopped up. "We could call it a …" She paused for dramatic effect. "… a Jammy Dodgy!"

"Squeak!" Boris gazed up at her adoringly.

"Teeny tiny." Fizzbee put her thumb and forefinger together.

"Ummm…" Scooter frowned. "Well, I think there might be something a bit similar already out there, but it's a great start. Just keep thinking along those lines and I'm sure you'll be able to come up with some more ideas."

"You're not so bad, Scooter McLay." Daffy grinned, before jotting it down in her book. "I just had an idea! Remember to share, Boris." She took the jam sandwich back from Boris, took a large bite, then passed him a blueberry.

"Phfff." She wafted her hand in front of her face. "Does jam inventing normally make you so hot? It's boiling in here, isn't it?"

As Scooter took another bite of his sandwich a bead of sweat dripped down his forehead. Daffy was right, it was getting a bit hot. A cloud of steam was rising from the water up ahead.

"Ooh." Cat dipped her toe in the water. "The water's lovely and warm! Anyone fancy a dip? Got any of those Banana Bubbles in RALPH, Scoot?" A funny feeling of dread came into the pit of Scooter's stomach as Cat continued. "It's about time old Captain DodgyBeard gave us something nice isn't it? After all, we've been chopped at, funnelled, added to sugar. Maybe he's decided it's time for us to have a bath!"

But Scooter didn't answer. Cat's words rang in his ears.

She was right. They'd been chopped, added to sugar and now water, too … just like fruit when you were making jam. But that meant that the next thing would be…

"Boiling!" Scooter gasped. "This isn't just a load of booby traps. It's a giant jam production unit! And we're the fruit!" He looked ahead, his eyes growing wide as he saw that the water was getting rougher. It was bubbling and burbling under a thick cloud of steam. A loud, churning noise was coming from somewhere ahead. "We have to get out of here!" he cried. "We're about to be *boiled*!"

CHAPTER ELEVEN

"But I thought if we knew how to make jam then we'd be OK!" Cat darted towards the edge of the boat, staring wildly at the rising steam ahead as Scooter scanned the walls desperately. They were totally smooth, just like the pipes that carried the jam around inside the factory. The ceiling was covered in small brass pipes but there was no way of reaching them.

His eyes met with Fizzbee's. She gave him a determined nod of understanding, then flew into the steam.

It wasn't long before she returned, her jam tart looking a little soggy and melty.

"Scooter!" She wiped a bead of sweat from her brow. "There is a whirlpool. The water is swirling and churning and bubbling! And it feels hot down there. It feels very, verrry hot."

Scooter gulped as he stared at the thickening steam. The churning noise was beginning to sound more like a roar.

He turned to look at each of his companions in the boat.

Daffy and Boris were clinging to each other for dear life.

Cat was flicking through her *How to Be a Spy* pocketbook as she searched desperately for an escape plan.

It was Fizzbee who acted first. She landed her jam tart in the centre of the boat and stretched her antennae out to the very edges.

"Fizzbee has seen a ledge ahead. It is near to the whirlpool, but Fizzbee will carry everyone to it."

She closed her eyes tight, took a deep breath and heaved with all of her might.

"Nnn𝐧𝐧𝐧𝐧ggggggggg𝐠𝐡𝐡hh𝐡𝐡𝐡hhh𝐡hh."

The boat rose millimetres from the water, then splashed back down again.

"It is verrrrry heavy." She took another deep breath and tried again.

"Nnn𝐧𝐧𝐧𝐧𝐧𝐧𝐧𝐧𝐧𝐧gggggg𝐆𝐠ggg𝐠𝐠ggggaa aa𝐚𝐚aahhhh𝐡𝐡𝐡𝐡𝐡𝐡𝐡hhh!"

This time the boat rose a centimetre.

"You're doing it, Fizz! Keep going!" Cat cheered her on as the boat inched towards the ledge, Fizzbee's face scrunching tighter with every excruciating second.

"She's not doing *that* well." Daffy peered over the edge of the boat. "I mean, we've barely moved!"

SPLOSH.

Fizzbee dropped them back down.

"Fizzbee has never carried anything this heavy before." She flopped back onto her jam tart. "If only Fizzbee had…" Her eyes lit up and she pulled her suitcase of inventions out of Scooter's pocket. "Anti-gravity powder!" She beamed, then gasped as the little suitcase fell out of her wet hands into the churning river below. She dived down as it bobbed along the water for a moment, then sank out of sight.

"Scooter!" she cried, her little face aghast. "What should Fizzbee *do*?"

"It's OK, I know what to do!" Cat shut her *How to Be a Spy* pocketbook with a determined nod.

She grabbed the rope from the front of the boat, untied it quickly, coiled it and threw it over her shoulder. She stood up, her legs slightly apart to steady herself, bent down and jumped with all of her might towards the pipes above, grabbing one by the tips of her fingers and pulling herself up until she had a firm grip on it.

She took a deep breath, then began swinging from one pipe to the other as if they were monkey bars, making her way steadily towards the ledge. As she reached it, she pulled her legs back, then forwards, then back, then somersaulted, landing feet first on the ledge.

"Quick, Fizzbee!" She took the rope from her shoulder and Fizzbee dashed towards her. "Get this to the boat!" She tied one end to a mooring ring on the floor as Fizzbee darted as fast as she could back towards Scooter.

Zing.

The rope went taut just a metre from the boat. Fizzbee pulled it again.

"Scooter!" she called. "This rope is too short!"

"What are we going to do?" Daffy shouted as they stared wide-eyed at the whirlpool ahead, the little boat gathering speed. "Oh Boris." She took a Jam Toilet Roll out of her pocket and dabbed Boris' forehead with it. "I think we might be goners." She pulled the roll away. "Urgh. It's all sticky."

"Daffy!" Scooter gasped. "You're a genius! The Jam Toilet Roll! Quick, chuck it into the water! Maybe it will block the whirlpool!" Daffy pulled more rolls out of her pocket and hurled them desperately into the sweet, sugary water, watching as they reached the edge of the whirlpool, swirling and whirling and twirling round and round and round and...

SLUUURRRPPLLEEE BuRRRBBBBLLLE SQUELCH SCHLOP.

Like a blocked toilet, the whirlpool slowed, bringing the boat to a perfect stop, right beside the little ledge.

"I saved us!" Daffy leapt out of the boat joyfully. "I did a good thing!" She stopped and wriggled her bum in jubilation, a confused look on her face. "It feels ... nice."

"Oh Scooter!" Fizzbee dived towards Scooter as he crawled out of the boat. "Fizzbee was so worried!"

"That was a bit close." Cat joined the hug.

"Squeak." Boris released a heart-shaped poo pellet.

"Look, Scooter." Fizzbee pointed to an arched stone passageway with a bright light shining from inside, one word chiselled into the stonework above it.

"That has to be the entrance to the treasure vault!" Scooter gasped. "We're finally here!"

"No way!" Cat hooted as Fizzbee circled Scooter's head in delight.

"You've only gone and found it!" Daffy gave him a playful shove and Boris squeaked with excitement.

"Come on!" Scooter beamed. "Let's go!"

Together, the little party walked slowly through the arch and down a stone staircase, away from the roar of the whirlpool and into an enormous cavern.

But not just any cavern.

A cavern *filled with more treasure than you could possibly imagine.*

Mounds and mounds of fat gold coins covered the floor.

Rubies as big as the juiciest strawberries were dotted amongst emeralds the size of luscious kiwis.

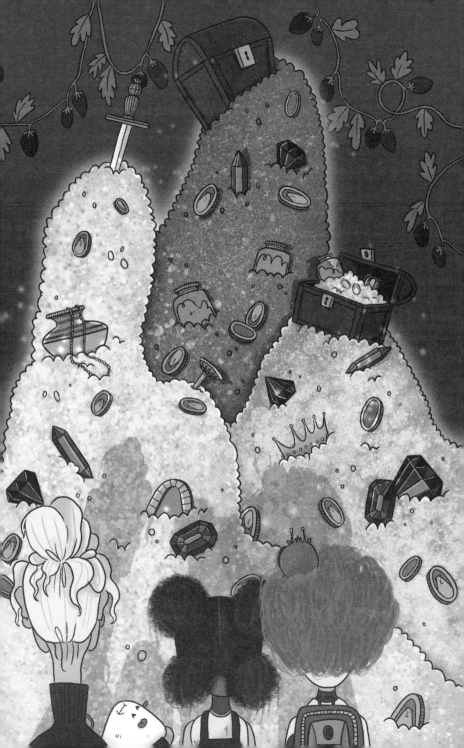

And then there was the jam.

The walls were stacked *full of it*!

Jars and jars of jam of every glittering colour.

"Whoa." Scooter and Fizzbee stepped forwards, their mouths hanging open. "This place is *amazing*!"

Daffy and Boris gawped in wonder at a vast statue of a giant golden guinea pig.

"That's Deadly Doris." Daffy looked down at Boris. "Your long lost relative."

"Squeak!" Boris snuffled towards a piece of paper folded at the bottom of the statue. Daffy picked it up and opened it.

*The **Perfect Wild Strawberry Jam**
by Captain Donald D. DodgyBeard*

"Boris!" Daffy squealed in delight. "You found Great Grandpa DodgyBeard's secret recipe!"

Scooter smiled and turned towards a large cone hanging down from the ceiling, the words JAMINATOR 500 written across it. There was a tap, switched to *Off*, at the side of it, and a line of jam jars on a conveyor belt below.

"This must be right below the whirlpool." He shook his head in amazement. "This whole place is a giant underground jam factory!" He looked up at a small beam of light shining down from above, revealing a trail of wild strawberry plants climbing the walls like vines. "He even grew his own strawberries, just like we do! That's incredible!"

"I can't believe we've actually found it!" Cat beamed as she looked at her watch. "And with plenty of time to spare. It's only 4 o'clock. You could even make it back in time for the Grand Reopening of *your* factory!" She clapped in delight. "The factory is safe. The treasure is with its rightful owner. All we need to do now is to stop Uncle Perry from sabot—" She noticed half a villainous moustache on the floor. She bent down to look more closely, then looked up, her eyes narrowing at the sight of a bucket on a rope hanging down from a tiny speck of light on the ceiling. "Scooter..." she whispered urgently. "My Uncle Perry – I don't know how but I think he might already be here!"

CHAPTER TWELVE

"Surprise!" Perry cha-cha-cha'ed out from the
shadows behind them while Colonel Pom Pom
clicked in time with the beat of his feet. Perry
twirled on the spot, did a step ball change and
finished with jazz hands. "I do like to make
an entrance!" he sneered gleefully at the five
utterly shocked faces in front of him.

"Oh, it's that nice health inspector." Daffy blushed and gave him a little wave. "Coo-eeee." Perry waggled his eyebrows attractively.

"Health inspector?" Scooter stared in surprise. "What health inspector? And what's he doing down here?"

"I think he might have a bit of a crush on me," Daffy whispered loudly as she patted her bun. "He's probably here to ask me out on a date."

"He's no health inspector." Cat stepped forwards. "He's my Uncle Perry and he's a low-down rotten *crook*!"

"I'm afraid it's true, my dear." Perry brushed down his velvet jacket and gave the remaining half of his moustache a villainous twizzle. "*And* I'm the owner of all of this treasure. After all, *I* found it first."

"**Meep.**" Colonel Pom Pom sniggered delightedly.

"But how did you…?"

"Oh, how did I get down here before you?" Perry interrupted. "Well, it wasn't part of the plan, I can tell you. But when I found out that you were planning to try and nab the treasure before me, I had to get here first. I thought it might be tricky, but then I heard that Daffy had taken over the factory again and I knew it wouldn't be too hard to charm my way inside." He turned to Daffy with his most oily smile. "No offence my dear, but you're not exactly the brightest spark. A little of the Pincher charm was all it took."

"Squeak!" Boris cried indignantly from inside the baby carrier as Daffy's chin dipped down, her ears flushed with embarrassment.

"As soon as we were inside, I just needed to lock Daffy away somewhere and let Colonel Pom Pom do his work. He can sniff out gold better than a shark can sniff out blood." He gave Colonel Pom Pom a little tickle under the chin and chuckled. "Nose of a genius, this one." Colonel Pom Pom wiggled his nose proudly and did a quick jig. "Quite right, Colonel Pom Pom. The nose of a genius and the feet of a ballerina." Perry patted him on the head fondly, then he and Colonel Pom Pom did a shimmy in perfect unison. "We're going to win the *One Owner and Their Pet Dance Championship*, don't you know? Anyway, Colonel Pom Pom knew we'd find the treasure at the bottom of the wishing well. Though goodness knows how he managed to sniff it out amongst all this reeking jam." Perry straightened the peg on the end of his nose.

"But that doesn't explain how you knew what we were planning. Or how you knew that Daffy was in charge. Have you been spying on me as well as stealing my stuff?" Cat stepped forwards, her hands on her hips.

"Perhaps you should ask Daffy about that." Perry sneered. "After all, I'd never have known if it wasn't for the jam-cam that she planted in your inventions lab."

"What?" Scooter's mouth fell open. "What jam-cam?"

"Oh, didn't you know?" Perry put his hand to his mouth as if he'd accidentally let out a secret. "Ooopsie. Anyway, enough of all this."

He pulled something out from his pocket and brandished it at them.

"I thought this might come in handy." He nodded towards a door that Scooter hadn't noticed before and lifted a bottle of water above the jar threateningly. "Now, all of you. In there."

"Popping Candy Jam?" Cat scoffed. "I'm not afraid of..."

"Stop!" Scooter put his hand out. "If that water gets near to that jam, it could bring the ceiling down on us all! Just do what he says." They backed slowly into the room.

"Don't worry." Perry turned to Scooter and Cat. "I'll leave a note for your parents once I'm gone. They'll come and find you in a week or two I expect."

"No!" Just as Cat ran towards the door, Perry slammed it shut in her face.

"Oh, and I nearly forgot!" They listened in horror as he turned the key in the lock. "I'm afraid there won't be much of a jam factory left when you get out." Perry gave the jar of Popping Candy Jam a little shake. "I've lived with that horrible stench for long enough." He clicked his heels. "I'd better start packing up my treasure now. Too-da-loo."

CHAPTER THIRTEEN

"You can't sabotage our factory!" Scooter banged on the door.

"Yes!" Fizzbee shouted loyally from her jam tart beside him. "And Scooter's jam smells delicious!" She kicked the door in frustration.

"Plus, you've never even tried it!" Cat shouted. "You should try things before you decide if you like them or not!"

"Squeak, squeak, squeak, squeak, squeak, squeak." Boris angrily held a blueberry aloft. "**SQUEAK!**"

SPLAT.

He squished the blueberry with his paw.

"This is *exactly* what Fizzbee was saying."
Fizzbee hovered down towards him. "But
Scooter says, Noooooo, Fizzbee. Nooooo
squishing like a bug." She rolled her eyes as
Boris nodded sympathetically.

"What was Perry saying about
a *jam-cam*?" Scooter rounded on
Daffy, then stopped as he looked at
her. She was sitting on an upturned
crate, her eyes red and blotchy.
Scooter couldn't help noticing how
sad she looked right now. Sad and
small and lonely. He sighed
and sat down beside her.
"What did you *do*?" he
asked, a little more calmly.

Daffy sniffed and wiped
her nose with the back of

her hand, then wiped her hand on her brown velour trousers.

"When I broke into your old factory," she started, "I wanted to steal all your secrets ... so, I planted a camera in your inventions room, but then—"

"You decided to go one better and let me build a new factory so you could steal that instead?" Scooter interrupted her with a roll of his eyes.

"I was going to say that I didn't think it worked. It was wedged behind some little suitcase with a sign on it that said DO NOT TOUCH UNDER ANY CIRCUMSTANCES. I decided it was probably for the best and I chucked the TV in a skip ages ago. I'd forgotten all about it until Perry mentioned it just now. He must have found the TV and seen when—"

"When we moved Fizzbee's suitcase of inventions earlier." Scooter finished her sentence for her.

"I guess so." Daffy sniffed. "I just wanted to be able to make amazing inventions like you." She stared hard at the floor. "Like my Great Grandpa DodgyBeard. But instead, I've messed everything up. All of this is my fault. I'm the one who tried stealing your factory. I'm the one who planted the jam-cam and revealed your plans to that crook and I'm the one who let him in. I've been such a silly fool." She scuffed her toe on a piece of dirt as Boris climbed onto her legs and snuggled into her lap sympathetically.

"You know, Uncle Perry was always planning to steal the treasure and sabotage the factory." Cat put her hand on Daffy's shoulder. "At least now, we have a chance to stop him." She turned to Scooter. "So, what's the plan, Scoot? How are we going to get out of here?"

"I don't think I *can* save the factory."

Scooter sighed heavily and looked at his watch. Nearly 5 p.m. "Just like I can't get back in time for the Grand Reopening." He swallowed hard as he pictured himself ready and waiting for the village to arrive. It would have been the best night of his life.

"It was going to be *amazing*. If they could see that I'm the Chief Inventor of the greatest jam factory in the universe, they'd see who I am! I've always had to keep everything a secret. When Fizzbee arrived, it felt so good not to hide my inventiveness. I wanted everyone to see what Fizzbee can see." His shoulders drooped. "But I guess they'll just carry on thinking that I'm nothing special after all."

"Scooter! Anyone who spends thirty seconds with you can see how brilliant you are!" Cat sat down beside him. "You don't need a Grand Reopening to prove that."

"This is true." Fizzbee nodded in agreement.

"It is not the factory that makes you special, Scooter. It is you that makes the factory special."

"Scooter, your inventions and ideas are so good that I've spent years trying to steal them. You can't give up now." Daffy pulled Captain DodgyBeard's secret recipe out of her pocket, together with her ideas notepad, and handed them to Scooter. "Here, have these. Maybe it's time I take a leaf out of Great Grandpa DodgyBeard's book and try to live a better life. You keep the factory. I won't try and steal it ever again. If you can save it from Perry, anyway," she added.

"Thanks." Scooter took the little notebook and the recipe. "But I don't have any of my inventions here. Well, apart from RALPH, I mean, and he's a bit broken." He gave RALPH a friendly pat and swallowed hard as a pile of sugar fell out of the little backpack onto his lap.

"But Scooter, great inventions come from great ideas," said Fizzbee. She hovered above them, her orange glow lighting the room. "And no one has ideas like Scooter. No one in this whole universe."

"That's right." Cat nodded. "And it wasn't your inventions that got us this far. It was your knowledge of jam! None of us would be here without that."

"Squeak." Boris nodded and released a little heart-shaped poo pellet.

Scooter looked around the room where

184

they sat. The walls were lined with dusty old jars of one-hundred-year-old jam, stacked one on top of the other. There were broken parts of machinery and a blackboard on the wall. A small wild strawberry plant trailed down from above. He looked at the pile of sugar on his lap, then at Daffy's ideas book and Captain DodgyBeard's secret recipe, his eyes lighting up.

"Did you say that Perry's never tried jam?" He turned to Cat with a grin.

"Scooter is having *ideas!*" Fizzbee squealed.

CHAPTER
FOURTEEN

Scooter stood beside the ancient blackboard as Fizzbee wrote a title in chalk.

HOW TO STOP PERRY FROM SABOTAGING THE FACTORY.

"The first thing we need to do is to get out of this room," Scooter explained.

"Scooter, I can pick the lock of that door easily." Cat pulled a hair clip out of her hair and Fizzbee drew a picture of it on the blackboard.

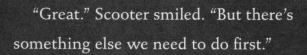

"Great." Scooter smiled. "But there's something else we need to do first."

"Oh." Cat put the clip back in her hair and Fizzbee rubbed out the drawing.

"We need to change Perry's mind about

jam." Scooter raised one eyebrow and gave them all a sage nod as Fizzbee drew a picture of Perry with a happy face and a speech bubble.

"Well, how in the heck are you ever going to do that?" Daffy frowned. "The man hates the stuff. And you can't give him *that*." She pointed to the one-hundred-year-old jars lining the wall.

"Cat said he's never tried it – but there's a first time for everything." Scooter grinned, pointing up to the wild strawberry plant as Hand-Bot Three extended from RALPH, a pile of sugar in its robotic hand. "We've got the ingredients right here to make *the best jam ever*. I mean, you said yourself that Captain DodgyBeard gave up his pirating for jam. Why not Perry, too? If we get him to try the best jam ever made, there's no way he'll ever want to sabotage our factory."

"Err…" Daffy pressed her lips together. "*That's* your plan? Give him some *jam*?"

"Squeak?" Boris put one paw over his face and closed his eyes with a long sigh.

"What if he doesn't like it?" Daffy tipped her head to one side. "And even if he does, what do you think's going to happen? He'll decide not to sabotage the factory and give up his life of crime while he's at it?"

"*Yes!* That's *exactly* what's going to happen!" Scooter threw his arms up in excitement.

Daffy, Boris and Cat blinked as Fizzbee drew another little speech bubble beside the picture of Perry.

"Err. I think we might have spoken a bit too soon about the whole amazing ideas thing," Daffy muttered to Boris.

"Leave the jam to me and Fizzbee." Scooter met each of their eyes, his chin held high. "Trust me. It'll work."

"He's probably got something a little extra to put in it – something *alieny*," Daffy whispered to Boris and Cat with a secret wink.

"But how are you going to get him to eat it?" Cat piped up. "Even with the peg on his nose, he can smell jam at twenty paces. There's no way you'll be able to trick him into trying it."

"That's where the next part of my plan comes in," Scooter explained. He placed RALPH on the floor in front of them.

"If you wouldn't mind helping a bit here?" He pressed the large orange button on the front and the team pulled and heaved as the little backpack creaked and croaked, groaned and grated, into a dented and dusty quad bike.

"It's going to take a bit of work." Scooter gave RALPH a sympathetic pat, then held up Daffy's notebook of ideas. "And we're going to need some really old jam."

"You're going to use my idea?" Daffy's whole face lit up.

"Yep." Scooter grinned. "Because it's a really good one. There's just one thing…" He paused. "We're also going to need a sock with a hole in it."

"No problem." Daffy began undoing her boots. "I've got just what you need."

"Excellent." Scooter beamed as the little group huddled together. "So, here's the plan."

In a flurry of activity, everyone got to work, making their preparations. Smoke billowed out as Daffy, Boris, Cat and Hand-Bot Three soldered, welded and wired, while Fizzbee and Scooter chopped, stirred, boiled and bottled to make the best jam ever tasted.

"I think that's everything." Scooter patted the newly adjusted RALPH as he held up a jar of freshly made jam.

"We're ready."

Back in the treasure vault, Perry and Colonel Pom Pom were practising their moonwalk as they packed treasure into their loot bags and piled them into the little tin bucket.

"I think we'll have to come back for the rest." Perry looked around at the magnificent chamber of treasure. "Let's go and sabotage the factory while we can." Colonel Pom Pom stopped twirling and sniggered delightedly. "A few drops of this in the machinery ought to do it." He pulled the little jar of Popping Candy Jam out of his pocket. "Once it's closed, we can walk back in whenever we like."

"A few drops of what, Uncle Perry?"

"Gah!" Perry jumped as Cat appeared with her hands on her hips in the doorway behind him. "Oh, it's you." He rolled his eyes. "I should have known you'd find a way out. Don't come any closer." He lifted the Popping

Candy Jam as Cat somersaulted towards him. "Actually, Uncle Perry –" she grabbed the little jar out of his hand as she cartwheeled past, landing on her plimsolls – "I think I'd better look after that."

"Oi!" Perry turned to her. "You can't just take that right out of my hand! That's stealing!"

"Oh, and by the way." Cat did a little step ball change. "You'd better cha-cha cha-nge where you're standing."

"What? Why?"

CRAAASSSHHHH—BLASSSSSSST

The ancient door exploded towards them.

"You're rumba-led." She beamed.

Perry's jaw dropped open as out rolled a gleaming orange *armoured tank*, the word RALPH emblazoned across it on a strip of painted fire. At the helm was Scooter, his red hair sticking up boldly from his head, and behind him sat Fizzbee, Daffy and Boris, their faces set in a grim line of determination, each of them holding their weapon of choice.

Fizzbee held a blueberry.

Daffy held a holey sock.

Boris held a cannon.

"We think it's about time that you tried some jam." Scooter smiled as Boris blasted the bucket full of pilfered treasure with one-hundred-year-old jam, sticking it to the spot.

"What do you think you're..." Perry spluttered as Daffy began to circle a sock above her head. It twirled round and round and round, gaining more and more momentum with every circuit. "A sock?" Perry sneered. "You're not seri..."

"Take that!" Daffy flung it with all of her might towards Perry.

SPLAT.

The sock hit the mark perfectly, right in his mouth.

"Argh glgggg bgggg," Perry gurgled in surprise as the sock dropped to the floor. *"Whgggg?"* He gulped, as a tiny globule of Strawberry Surprise Jam passed down his throat and into his belly with an uncomfortable glug.

Perry's moustache twitched.

Then it twitched again.

"What *was* that?" he whispered, his hand held to his chest.

"That –" Scooter smiled – "was Strawberry Surprise Jam." He held up the jar.

"But..." Perry looked a bit mushy as he rolled his tongue around his mouth. "It's wonderful!" He twirled on the spot. "Oh, it's sweet and yummy and sticky and scrummy!" He picked up the holey sock from the floor, dipped his finger into a blob of remaining jam, then licked it appreciatively. "Colonel Pom Pom, you have to try this! How could we ever consider sabotaging a factory that could make something as wonderful as *this*?"

"Errrr..." Daffy nudged Scooter. "How come that worked? Did you find some more of those Friendship Sprinkles somewhere?"

"Nope." Scooter grinned.

"Then what did you put in it?" Daffy asked as Scooter held up the jar for her to see.

STRAWBERRY SURPRISE

"Actually, I used one of your inventions." Scooter raised his eyebrows. "The surprise is that there's no surprise. It's just strawberry jam." He glanced up at the wild strawberry plants on the walls. "The best jam comes from the freshest fruit. It turns out that even Captain DodgyBeard knew that secret!"

All five of them – Scooter, Fizzbee, Cat, Daffy and Boris – watched as Perry and Colonel Pom Pom began waltzing around the cavern.

"You know what, Colonel Pom Pom?" Perry grinned. "I think we should give up the life of crime!"

"**Meep!**" Colonel Pom Pom squealed delightedly as he leapt into Perry's outstretched arms for a magnificent lift.

Daffy's jaw
dropped.

"Jam
is verrrry
powerful."
Fizzbee nodded
sagely.

"It *really* is."
Cat giggled as
Scooter looked
at his watch.

17:00.

"Five minutes
until the Grand
Reopening." He
sighed. "I guess
we've missed it now."

"I'm sorry, Scooter." Daffy put her arm on
his shoulder.

"We can help you plan another one when

199

we're back." Cat stood the other side of him.

CRREEEEEAAAAAAAAAKKKKKKKKKKK.

They turned towards the JAMINATOR 500.

It was bulging a bit.

Actually, it was creaking, and groaning and ballooning at an alarming rate. Almost as though something inside was blocking it.

GRRROOAAWOHRROooWWWWWNGGGGNGNGNAAAAK

"The Jam Toilet Rolls!" Scooter cried. "We blocked the JAMINATOR but it's still trying to make jam! Quick, we need to switch it off before it…"

KABOOOOOOOOOOOO

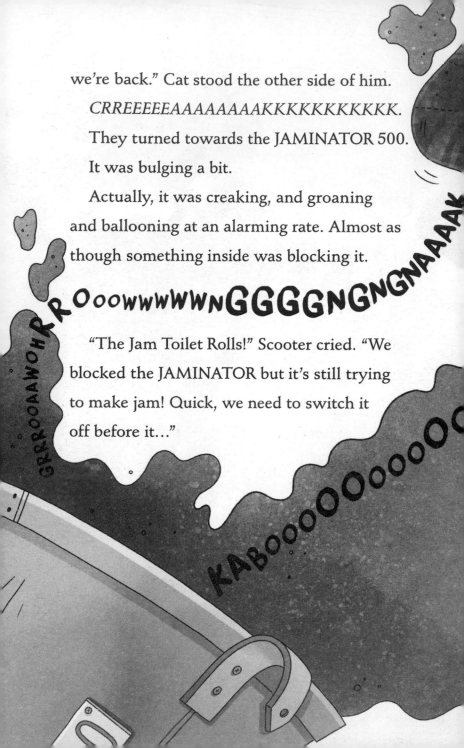

CHAPTER FIFTEEN

The JAMINATOR
500 exploded and a
mixture of Jam Toilet Roll,
sugary water and old jam began
ferociously pouring into the cavern like a
tidal wave, filling the doorways and blocking
every exit within seconds.

"Oh no!" Scooter watched as the water
covered his toes, his feet, his knees and
continued to pour into the room, the gold
and jewels sinking below it.

"We need to get out of here!" he cried, just as a small suitcase bobbed past him. A small suitcase covered with the words DO NOT TOUCH UNDER ANY CIRCUMSTANCES.

"Fizzbee!" He gestured towards it and Fizzbee dived down to pick it up.

"Quickly, everyone onto RALPH!" Scooter shouted as Fizzbee hovered back towards him. "We'll need to use your anti-gravity invention, Fizz."

"Yes, Scooter." Fizzbee grinned as she began sprinkling the silver powder all over RALPH.

Meanwhile, the villagers of Willowden Green buzzed with excitement as they gathered outside the doors of the new jam factory.

5.58 p.m.

Almost time for the Grand Reopening to begin!

Except ... something funny was going on.

Something weird.

The factory was in absolute darkness.

Almost as if there was no Grand Reopening.

Hushed whispers raced around the crowd.

"Maybe their magic ran out," whispered little George Baker.

"I think they've been taken by aliens," piped up Oti Messoud.

"You're both wrong," snapped Lucy Dunning. "They've been employed by Father Christmas. They've packed up and left for the North Pole."

"Has anyone actually tried the front door?" joined in that clever boy, Joshua Small.

The crowd all turned to look at the front door as the Mayor straightened his livery collar and stepped forwards. He gave the crowd a reassuring smile and knocked firmly on the front door.

Rat-a-tat-tat.

Nothing.

The Mayor smiled again, coughed, and pushed it.

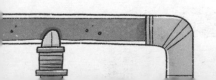

"By golly, the boy's right!" he cried as the front door opened and, like a herd of hungry goats, the villagers swept into the dark factory, wondering what magical surprise might be in store for them next.

At exactly the same moment, Scooter's parents arrived back from their trip to the lawyers. Tired and deflated, they turned off the dirt track, only to discover an enormous group of excited villagers dressed in ball gowns and tuxedos filing into the dark factory.

"Why are the factory lights all off?" Scooter's mum frowned. "You don't think it's anything to do with Scooter and Fizzbee, do you?" They joined the back of the queue.

"Daffy's not even here!" Scooter's dad exclaimed as they reached the wishing well. "Maybe we should tell everyone to go back home. I … errr … excuse me?" He stood on the edge of the wishing well. "I'm afraid that the err … Grand Reopening…" The villagers listened intently. "Well, it's cancel—" The well began to shake and stutter below him, and he stopped talking.

What on earth was happening?

SWWwoOOOOooOSHHHHHHHH!

Everyone watched in rapturous wonder as a bright orange armoured tank rocketed into the factory above their heads.

They gazed as it hovered for a moment, blanketed by a soft orange glow while Scooter

McLay, the boy who actually lived at the jam factory, smiled out at them.

"Welcome to McLay's Jam!" He beamed as a small alien inside a jam tart flew out from a cup holder.

"The most stupendous jam factory in the world!" Fizzbee grinned shyly.

"It really is!" Cat floated out from behind the quad bike and Perry and Colonel Pom Pom pirouetted in mid air.

The entire village fell into ecstatic applause.

"But don't even think about stealing anything from it." Daffy stared down menacingly from where she and Boris sat astride a tiny flying cannon.

The clock struck 6.00 p.m. and right on cue, the pre-programmed giant robotic tools and machinery began serving Lemon Jam Fizz to drink, glow-in-the-dark jam sandwiches, Bubble Gum Jam Sausages and Smoking Strawberry Jam Ice Cream to the gaggle of thrilled villagers.

"Fizzbee is thinking that Scooter has blown the villagers' pants right off with this entrance." Fizzbee grinned.

"I think you mean socks." Scooter giggled.

"Scooter!" As RALPH came to land on the factory floor, his parents ran over and hugged him hard. "What's going on?" They turned to

look at Perry, Colonel Pom Pom and Cat.
Then Daffy and Boris.

"Don't worry," Scooter reassured them,
Fizzbee hovering beside him as always.
"Everything's going to be OK."

"Yes, don't you worry." Daffy slid down
from the tiny floating cannon and popped
Boris safely back into the baby carrier. She put
her arms around Scooter's parents. "Let your
old pal Daffy explain it all to you."

CHAPTER SIXTEEN

McLay's JAM

One Month Later...

Scooter watched as a huge crane lifted down the *Dodgy ~~Doughnuts~~ Jam* sign from the top of the Dodgy Tower and replaced it with another.

McLay's Jam.

"Great Grandpa DodgyBeard would be pleased to have a true jam maker taking over." Daffy proudly straightened her new *Head of Security* hat as she took a bite of a Jammy Dodgy biscuit. "But I still think Dodgy Jam was a much better name."

"Squeak." Boris's head poked out of the baby carrier. He was wearing a shining *Deputy of Security* collar.

"Come on, Boris." Daffy patted the sock tucked in her belt. "Let's make another round and check the factory is secure."

"Squeak." Boris held up his jam cannon threateningly.

"Scooter!" Fizzbee hovered towards them eagerly, a spoon of jam in her little hand.

"What's this, Fizz?" Scooter smiled.
"Another new invention?"

"It's Floating Fig." Cat hovered just behind
her. "You've got to try it!"

It hadn't been easy to persuade Mum and Dad to let Fizzbee use her alien inventions. But, in Scooter's typically determined way, he'd refused to take no for an answer. As far as he was concerned, Fizzbee had as much right to work on her inventions as he had to work on his. As soon as the Grand Reopening was over, he'd spent night and day telling them all about how Fizzbee's inventions had in fact saved his life *and* helped to save their factory. In the end they had wearily agreed. But only on the express understanding that all of Fizzbee's inventions must undergo a strict testing process before they were added to *any* of McLay's jams.

Cat had readily agreed to be a taste tester.

"Ooh. Can I try some?" Daffy peered down at the spoon in Fizzbee's hand. "That'll help me and Boris tonight at our *One Owner and Their Pet* dance classes. I was wondering how we were going to manage the new lift."

"Squeak." Boris nodded, a slightly relieved look on his little face.

Perry and Colonel Pom Pom had decided not to leave town after all. They didn't want to move too far away from the factory, now that they'd discovered jam. Instead, they had set up a brand new (and surprisingly popular) *One Owner and Their Pet* dance studio in the village of Willowden Green. Daffy and Boris had been the first to sign up.

One Owner and Their Pet
EVERY FRIDAY
AT WILLOWDEN
VILLAGE HALL

DANCE STUDIO

"Look, Scoot!" Mum walked towards them, proudly waving a newspaper article in the air. Dad followed behind, chatting with Cat's parents as they carried a huge picnic basket between them.

"You're in the news *again*!" Mum held up the newspaper for him to see and gave his hair a proud ruffle.

McLay's Jam, it's out of this world! What will Chief Inventor at McLay's jam factory, Scooter McLay, and his best friend, Fizzbee, come up with next? Only time will tell, but this reporter for one, can't wait to find out!

Below it was a smiling picture of Scooter in his lab coat, Fizzbee hovering by his shoulder as always.

"Ready for the picnic, Scoot?" Dad asked.

"Yep." Scooter grinned as he sat astride a bright orange quad bike, RALPH2 emblazoned across it on a splodge of jam. Fizzbee hovered down into the jam tart holder and Cat climbed aboard beside him.

Hand-Bot Three reached out to flip open
a hidden control panel and Scooter pressed a
new button.

FLIGHT MODE.

"Ready?" Scooter beamed and together they
soared into the sky.

The End

What is cerebral palsy?

The hero of this book, Scooter McLay, has cerebral palsy. This is a condition that affects his movement and muscle control. The messages between his brain and his body can get a little jumbled or lost.

Cerebral → brain
Palsy → difficulty with controlling muscles, and therefore movement, in the body

Cerebral palsy can affect different parts of the body.

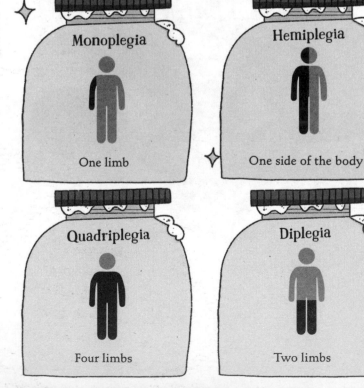

Monoplegia

One limb

Hemiplegia

One side of the body

Quadriplegia

Four limbs

Diplegia

Two limbs

For Scooter, it means that the muscles on the left side of his body are a little stiff and he wears a splint on his left leg to give him extra support to allow him to stand and walk more easily. However, cerebral palsy affects every person differently.

Cerebral palsy affects around 1 in 400 children born in the UK

These are the main types of cerebral palsy:

Spastic cerebral palsy
This is the most common type. Spasticity makes the muscles tight and stiff, reducing movement.

Dyskinetic (athetoid) cerebral palsy
Dyskinetic cerebral palsy causes uncontrolled body movements and can affect speech or language.

Ataxic cerebral palsy
Ataxia makes balance and co-ordination difficult, leading to shaky movements. This can affect speech and language.

PEOPLE WITH CP HAVE IT ALL THEIR LIVES

Cerebral palsy can cause problems with movement, breathing, balance, sleeping, eating, posture, hearing, sight and communication

Make your own jammy biscuits

Ingredients

80g caster sugar
175g soft butter
225g plain flour
Jam – your choice
of flavour

Remember to
ask an adult
to help with
the oven

Equipment

Bowl
Rolling pin
2 baking sheets
  greased and lined with
  greaseproof paper
Scales
Cooling rack
Wooden spoon
Teaspoon
Cutters: 7cm round and
  4cm round

1. Preheat oven to 160°c/140°c fan/gas 3.

2. Beat the sugar and butter in a bowl until smooth
   and fluffy, then add the flour and stir until mixed.
   Use your hands to form two balls of dough.

3. Put one ball of dough between two sheets of
   greaseproof paper and, using a rolling pin, roll
   out until 5mm thick. Using the bigger cutter,
   cut out your biscuits. Re-roll any leftover dough
   and repeat. You should have 8/10 biscuits.

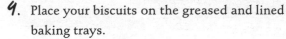

4. Place your biscuits on the greased and lined baking trays.

5. Repeat step three with the second ball of dough. Using the smaller cutter, cut out the middle of your biscuit and place on the baking trays.

6. Chill in fridge for 10 minutes on the trays.

7. Bake for 12–15 minutes until light golden. Cool on tray for 5 minutes and then carefully lift onto a cooling rack.

8. When your biscuits feel cold, spread the jam (approx. 1tsp each) onto the whole biscuits and then place the second, cut out, biscuits on top of the jam to make a sandwich.

9. Ta-da! You've done McLay's jam factory proud! Now enjoy eating your delicious jammy biscuits!

This extremely yummy recipe has been developed by McLay's jam factory consulting chefs, Lucy and Edith Longlade

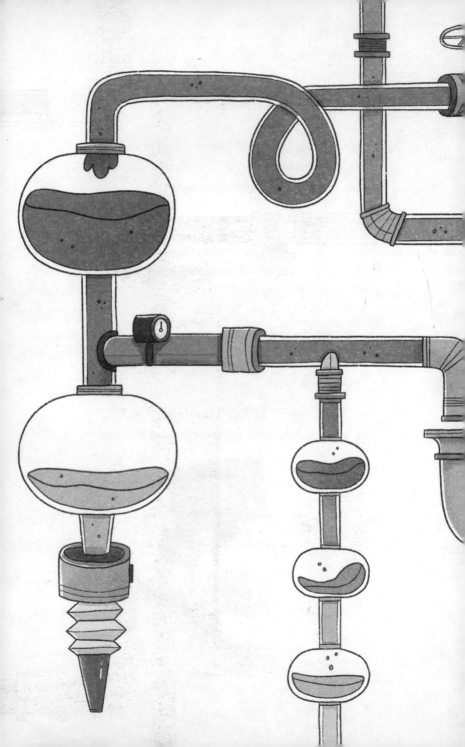

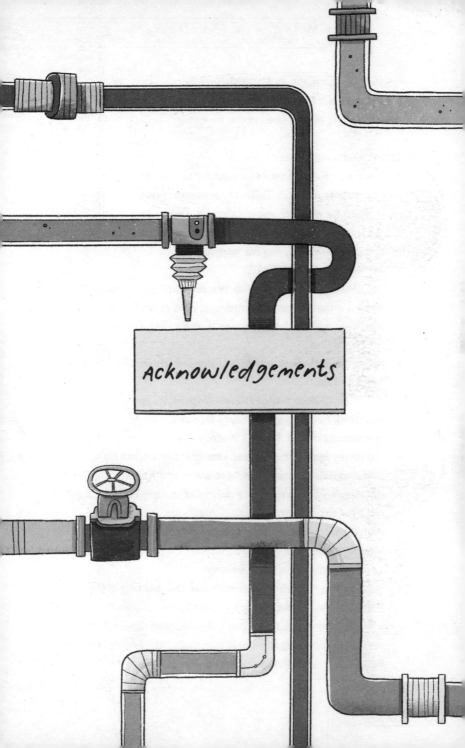

Writing a book is much like searching for treasure. You need a map, a lot of determination and most importantly, special people to join you on the adventure.

Thank you so much to:

- My agent Kate Shaw, who is quite simply jamtastic.
- My editors, Frances Taffinder and Non Pratt. I couldn't have wished for a better, more talented, fun or lovely pair to work with in bringing Scooter and Fizzbee's second adventure into the world. Thank you for jampioning me and for all your brilliant notes and ideas.
- All of the jamazing team at Walker books and especially design wizard, Jamie Hammond, who sprinkles magic into the pages of books, much like Fizzbee's potions on Scooter's jam.
- Jenny Taylor – best and most talented illustrator EVER. You are The Jam.
- All of my fellow writer friends (especially my Golden Egg buddies), book bloggers, Insta-jam and Twitter pals. Special thanks to Jen and Toby O'Brien.
- All of my lovely friends and jamily – I wouldn't be here without you. Special thanks to Lucy and Edith Longlade for developing and testing the delicious jammy biscuit recipe (and for the biscuit delivery – yum).
- Abigail, my goddaughter, who continues to inspire Scooter's jam-ventures. And her mum, Carrie, for her insightful feedback and friendship. You are awesome.
- And finally, my wonderful husband and our two children, Meg and Hattie. For always getting involved when I blurt out a random new jam flavour in the middle of dinner, for never tiring of discussing my latest plot quandary and for always laughing at my rubbish jam puns. You jamplete me.